Michael Sala was born in the Netherlands and first came to Australia as a child in the 1980s. He lives in Newcastle on the New South Wales north coast. He is the author of two novels, *The Last Thread* and *The Restorer*. *The Last Thread*, his critically acclaimed debut, was winner of the New South Wales Premier's Award for New Writing and regional winner of the Commonwealth Book Prize in 2013.

MICHAEL
SALA

THE LAST THREAD

TEXT PUBLISHING MELBOURNE AUSTRALIA

textpublishing.com.au

The Text Publishing Company
Swann House
22 William Street
Melbourne Victoria 3000
Australia

First published by Affirm Press, 2012
This edition published by The Text Publishing Company, 2017

Cover design by Sandy Cull, gogoGingko
Image by David Lichtneker/Arcangel
Page design by Jessica Horrocks
Typeset by Affirm Press/J&M Typesetting

Printed in Australia by Griffin Press, an Accredited ISO AS/NZS 14001:2004 Environmental Management System printer.

National Library of Australia Cataloguing-in-Publication entry
Creator: Sala, Michael, author.
Title: The last thread/by Michael Sala.
ISBN: 9781925498516 (paperback)
ISBN: 9781925410754 (ebook)
Subjects: Families—Australia—Fiction. Dutch—Australia—Fiction. Family secrets—Australia—Fiction. Netherlands—Fiction. Australia—Fiction.

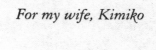

For my wife, Kimiko

BERGEN OP ZOOM

1

Television on. Living room swims in light and noise. The *shhh* from the speakers sounds like rain, so loud you can't hear the drops. The corridor is dark. Michaelis stops his tricycle at the bedroom door. His face makes a ghost in the orange gleam. He reaches up and rattles the handle. He hears them on the other side, Dad and his brother, and he calls out. The door doesn't open.

'One day, you'll have a face like this.'

When Dad smiles, his nose curves, and you can see hair in his nostrils, a tiny forest of it. He trims it sometimes in the mirror in the hallway, but it always grows back. They ride on a pushbike, Michaelis at the front, on the bar between Dad's arms, Constantine at the back. They ride alongside a field locked in early morning fog. The ears of rabbits rise and dip as the bike rattles past.

'You always say they're rabbits,' Dad says, 'but they're not. They're hares. Hares have longer ears.'

Smoke plumes from the factory in the distance. The air smells of yoghurt. Dad's arms tense with each push against the pedals. He wears a black leather jacket that smells like an animal. The leather folds and shines in the crook of his elbows.

In the park, Constantine and Dad pass a ball between them with stabs of their feet. Dad talks about how he used to be the star player in the army back in Cyprus.

'This is what I used to be good at. You should have seen me.'

'Where's Cyprus, Dad?'

'Oh, a long, long way off.' Dad talks to Michaelis from the side of his mouth. 'Concentrate on the ball. Pass it to him, Constantinos.'

Con can turn on the ball and kick it to exactly where he wants. He's pretending there are players around him, ready to fight for the ball, but there's no one.

Michaelis runs between him and Dad, waving his arms. When the ball comes his way he trips over it. Dad helps him up and points to the inside of his foot. 'This is where you hit the ball. That's the sweet spot, where you control it. Just look, really look. See?'

Michaelis doesn't. The ball skids off, and Dad follows. 'Constantinos, see if you can take the ball from me.'

Constantinos. That's how they say it back in Cyprus.

Dad is panting now, working the ball from foot to foot, talking only to Con. 'Do you know why Holland lost, Constantinos? They didn't have Cruyff. That's why Argentina beat them. But one day, in the World Cup, Holland will have *you*.'

Con steals the ball. As he runs, the ball skims over his heel and spills out in front and he guides it away.

'Ah, Constantinos,' says Dad, standing in his wake, bowed over, hands on his knees. Then he straightens and turns. 'Micha-ayleees! Don't go too close to the water!'

Michaelis doesn't know if he is drawn to the pond or bored by the game. Water ripples around the reeds. Something splashes at the corner of his gaze. He turns and waits. It doesn't come again. Dad is trying to catch Con. He runs out of breath and begins laughing and coughing all at once. He says he should stop smoking, but smiles as he puts his jacket back on and takes a cigarette out from the inside pocket.

Constantine stands apart, juggling the ball, making no sound but the echo of leather and air. Michaelis swears that ball will never touch the ground. When it does, Con simply scoops it up with his toes and flicks it to the other foot like nothing happened. The wind lifts his hair and lets go. Dad looks at Constantine as if he has forgotten to tell him something and Michaelis watches Dad, his face hollow at the cheeks, his paper-thin eyelids, and his teeth pulling at his bottom lip. It is fascinating, the look of the smoke unravelling into the air from his mouth, like knots coming undone.

They ride into town along the bicycle path. Naked trees separate the path from a road gleaming with afternoon traffic. Houses huddle together on the other side, bay windows shielded by small gardens. Once Mum told Michaelis about how she used to stop outside windows when she was a little girl. She'd stop on her way home from school and stand there all by herself. She did this when someone had died inside.

'The curtains were drawn for three days. That's how you knew. I'd stand in front of the curtains and feel sad for them inside. No, not sad, but I wanted to share their sadness.'

Even when Mum isn't close to him, her stories are.

They pass through a cluster of trees, along another park and into the heart of town. The salmon-pink path is a blur beneath them. Dad's shoes catch the light with each turn. People queue at the stand in front of the closed department store for newspapers and thick red lengths of boiled sausage. The man hands them over in white paper bags full of steam. *Rookworst*. At the first bite, the juices squirt out and burn the back of your throat. When they go there, Michaelis only ever gets a small piece, but it's rich and salty and he never finishes it.

The Pepper Shaker rises ahead: the grey stone cathedral with a clock face in the sky, its roof narrowing to a spire pressing like a needle against the clouds. They ride past it, across the cobble-stoned market square and stop at Crusio, the ice-cream shop. Crystal bowls are stacked in the window, brimming with balls of ice-cream that never melt, swirls of chocolate, wafers and thin tubes of biscuit. The door opens and warm air spills over them, full of waffles and coffee. Voices echo amid the creak of chairs and scraping spoons and laughter. A smiling lady behind the counter carves them their own mountain. Michaelis eats until he's sick. It's the middle of the day, though you wouldn't know it from the rain drizzling onto the polished stones.

Dad hunches over the table in his leather jacket and wipes his mouth with a napkin. 'You boys have to go home soon.'

From the beginning, when Michaelis first sees him, he knew this would happen.

Dad drops them at the front door, stays on his bike and chats with Mum. Michaelis watches them talk from inside the doorway, Dad's skin very dark next to Mum's, the nervous twitch in Mum's hands and her eyes. Then Dad is off, weaving his bike back and forth across the path. He winks over his shoulder as he rides away.

'Did you have a good time?'

'Oh, yes,' Michaelis answers.

Constantine is already gone.

'It's true.'

Mum stirs on the couch, fingers wrapped around a cup of coffee in her lap. She is staring out the window. The coffee is cold. She tastes it, frowns, and puts it on the table. 'Your brother is right. We *did* live together once.

7

We lived together in London. And in Cyprus, on top of a hill with no running water or electricity. But it had such a view! Your dad's parents brought out a jar of sparrows when I arrived. They were plucked bare and pickled in the vinegar, and your grandparents wanted me to eat one, beak and all.'

She makes a face. Michaelis can see the gums of her teeth, pink and clean. Her upturned nose grows small between her large blue eyes. She smells of patchouli, a mossy, rich scent. You can smell it in the house when she walks from one part of it to the other. It's in all her clothes.

'Oh, God, those naked little sparrows. It made me sick to the stomach just looking at them!'

'I remember that,' Michaelis says.

'You don't remember anything.' Constantine is standing in the doorway, watching them. 'We were together, Michaelis, until you came along.'

'And after,' Mum says softly. 'For a while after.'

They lived together in London and then in Cyprus, with its mountains full of dark-skinned relatives and blue sky and bright oranges and narrow, dusty trails. It's true: Michaelis can't remember much from back then, but he knows the stories. And when he listens to Mum, it's like he really *can* remember.

An old woman lives in Cyprus in a stone house on top of a hill that looks out to the sea. She makes treats:

almonds threaded together with string, encased in a pale tea-coloured sheath, like a length of hose. They taste sweet, full of strange spices, and the almonds make a paste in your mouth that you need a drink of water to swallow down. The almond chains reach Dad by mail. When the boys visit him, he hands them over coiled up in an old ice-cream container.

'From your grandmother,' he says.

Although the taste makes him queasy, Michaelis eats as much as he can. It is all he knows of this woman.

~

Boiled potatoes tumble into a silver strainer over the sink. There are scars in the metal. Steam gathers around Mum, and she smiles, running her fingers back and forth across her apron.

Crouching in front of him, she takes one of his hands in her own. 'They're like mine, you know, and like your grandfather's. Artistic.'

Mum straightens, drops the potatoes back into the pot and begins crushing them into mash, pausing to drizzle over the fat from thinly sliced bacon and onions that she has just fried.

'You were blue. That's how poor we were in London. We couldn't afford the heating. We lived in a tiny flat. The place was fine in the summer, but the winter was cold and went on forever, and you cried and cried. One wall was constantly damp. You were unhappy, sick all the time. You never slept well. Your dad was hardly there. Sometimes I had to go out and walk the streets all by myself—I couldn't listen to your crying.'

Her arms work at the potato masher, her bare, red elbows bent outwards. She pauses to drop in some salt. Add a pinch of this. Stir. Taste.

Her stories are strange and often sombre, but magical too. Michaelis can listen to the same ones again and again. It's like touching stuff that doesn't exist. Fairytales. He can imagine Mum walking the streets. She has this desperate look sometimes, where her chin tightens, her head tilts to one side, and her movements get jerky. You can hear it in her steps.

'And your brother didn't want you there. Soon as you were born, he tried to bury you. He would throw things in your cot. Shoes, jackets, toys, anything he could find. I came in one day and couldn't even see your face.'

Michaelis remembers one thing about London. He remembers standing in his cot and rattling the wooden bars, crying. The insides of his ears hurt. Some time, before or after that, Mum gives him a tablet, which tastes sour. This was when Dad lived with them, and now that time is gone.

Dad lives somewhere else. He smells of expensive aftershave, and every hair on his head is in place. His skin feels rough, especially when you go against the grain, as if there is sand under the surface. Dad laughs and winks and everything is a joke, and when the boys are at his house, in the mornings, he chases them on all fours in his pyjamas, which flap around his wiry body. He likes to wrestle with them, too, until sometimes the games go on without Michaelis, and he is left in the living room or listening from the corridor.

When Dad chases them, he calls them animals, but he lengthens and bends the last part of the word. 'Animaaales,' he exclaims. 'You are both animaaales!' The words come to Michaelis between his own shrieking laughter, between trying to get away from Dad and rolling with him on the floor.

Then he is gone.

There is someone else in their family—Dirk: larger than Dad, heavier, without jokes. You can hear him moving a mile off, his breath and the plod of his workboots, his sigh and the creak of his belt when he sits down. Michaelis carries his last name. To make things easy, Mum says. But Michaelis can't even spell that name. There are too many letters.

Dirk has a thick beard, large hands and corduroy pants that sag beneath his belly. His pipe moves from one corner of his mouth to the other. He smells of tobacco and leather and wood shavings. His black hair is short and curly across his large head.

On the weekend, Dirk works in the shed at the end of the back garden. When he works, his mouth disappears into his beard. He makes furniture and occasionally toys out of wood. He leans over the wood, a long, heavy chisel angled beneath his tar-stained fingers, and things get made. 'The cleverness of the man,' Mum says. Sometimes he hammers things together and hits his own finger, cursing in a voice that rattles the inside of Michaelis's head.

~

The clouds are dark grey, like the concrete from the wall is seeping into the sky. Michaelis rides a go-kart, while the boy behind him pushes. Michaelis doesn't pay attention and steers into the wall. The boy behind him doesn't pay attention either, and keeps pushing.

One of Michaelis's fingers gets wedged between concrete and metal and splits open. He screams. The go-kart stops and he sits there, staring at the wound. It is beginning to rain, light drops drifting onto his cheeks. A curled leaf of skin hangs from his finger. The tears do not come straight away. The blood holds back. Both come out at once, and then he can't stop. He is bleeding and wailing like he was made for it. A fascinated ring of children bustles closer.

The tomatoes are swollen and dark red. Mum runs a knife along each one before she drops it into boiling water. A thin cut in the flesh, barely visible. The skin of the tomato unfurls when it hits the water, like a flower blooming. Michaelis is standing on a chair, holding the benchtop for balance, looking down at the pot on the stove, watching Mum work.

'When Constantine was your age, maybe a bit younger, about three, he got his first bike. It had training wheels.'

Michaelis's bike has training wheels too.

'Constantine absolutely refused to ride the bike until we took them off. I don't think he wanted the other kids to see him needing those wheels. He fell over a few times, but he kept going. He doesn't like help, your brother.'

'Why?'

Mum shrugs. 'He just never has. He's always been his own man. When he was two, when Moessie visited, he got everyone water. He insisted on doing that by himself, too. Brought it out for us one after the other, in the same cup, like we were at church. We drank and only then did we wonder *how* he got the water. My father followed him into the bathroom. He was getting it from the toilet bowl.'

Mum tells these stories when Dirk isn't around, when she has visitors. She goes on telling the stories when the visitors are gone, when it is just Michaelis and her, when Constantine is at school and they drink tea and listen to music on the record player, or when she is cooking dinner.

'Your brother used to write on the walls when he was little. He'd do these sprawling murals from one end of the wall to the other. He'd use his own poo. Very involved, he was. He stuffed the poo into his toys as well. He had this small red double-decker bus. I don't know how he got the poo all the way to the back. It must have taken him a long time.'

Listen. The look on Mum's face is more important than the story, but listen to every word and try to give her more. Put yourself inside the stories, so that the laughter can be about you.

'Start here,' Michaelis says.

'I don't know.' Sebastiaan looks away. Every time he breathes, a bubble of snot comes out of his nose before shrinking back inside. Mum and Dirk are drinking coffee with Sebastiaan's parents downstairs. The boys are upstairs, where it is quiet.

Sebastiaan's room is full of strange toys that Michaelis doesn't own himself—a Godzilla nearly as long as his arm, a tub of green slime, a narrow plank on wheels called a skateboard, a bunch of Playmobil cowboys and Indians—but he's grown tired of them. Now he wants to make a trail of poo from one end of Sebastiaan's room all the way to the stairs and down them, if they have enough ammunition.

'Come on, Sebastiaan.'

'I don't know.' He says it now in a soft, whining tone.

'It's now or never,' Michaelis tells him.

Mum said this not long ago about going to live somewhere else. She said it to Dirk back home, at night, in the living room when she thought Michaelis was asleep. Michaelis likes the sound of those words, the shape of them. *Now or never.* Downstairs, he can hear Mum. She'll come up sooner or later; she always comes in the end when things are quiet. Sebastiaan pulls down his pants. They work in silence. Squat, squeeze, hold, then a careful shuffle forward, pants still around the ankles. It is easy until they reach the stairs. The stairs need great balance. It's like a circus act. Michaelis nearly falls onto his face. He's running out of ammo. Before he can get to the second step, a shadow falls across him. Dirk says one thing. '*Verdomme.*'

Things happen very quickly after that.

Michaelis's head hurts all the way home. His right ear throbs with heat. Mum and Dirk are quiet in the front of the car. Constantine is grinning beside him, tapping a finger softly on the bottom of the window so that only Michaelis can hear.

'*Verdomme,*' Dirk says again. His shoulders tense and his hands clench the steering wheel. '*Verdomme.*'

This is what he says when he is angry. And when he is really angry, Dirk says *godverdomme*. You want to be as far away as possible when he says that. The *g* is thick and heavy, because Dirk pulls it from every part of his lungs. It's an angry thing that sleeps in Dirk's stomach, and when he isn't angry, he speaks in a low voice, as if he doesn't want to wake it.

~

'I hope you'll remember this.'

Mum turns away to face the cathedral. The market square is full of people. More are pouring in from the narrow streets. Voices and music swollen with cymbals and trumpets bounce off the painted stone shopfronts and restaurants. The buildings gazing down on the square are crowded with tall rectangular windows, some shuttered, most dark.

Michaelis floats above the commotion on Dirk's shoulders. Everyone wears a costume. Even the Pepper Shaker, the grey cathedral rising from the buildings ahead, is dressed in blue sheets that snap and billow in the wind. The Pepper Shaker leans against the sky with vast, creaking arms of wood covered in canvas, and a grinning face on the clock at the top of the tower.

Dirk points at the Pepper Shaker and speaks around his pipe. 'He's a farmer today. *Een boer.*'

The ball of tangled tobacco in the chute of his pipe glows red and withers. Michaelis also smokes a pipe, except his pipe is made of candy. A procession is emerging from one of the side streets, orange flags and giant heads floating and swaying above the crowd. Over the angled

16

rooftops, between the clouds, the moon makes a face. Poor moon, drowning in a daytime sky. Mum was crying this morning, in her bedroom, but when she came out, she was smiling and too busy to talk.

Michaelis's fingers hook in the black curls of Dirk's hair. The layers of muscle and flesh in Dirk's shoulders tremble when he coughs or laughs. People are singing. Nearby stands a wooden carriage, its sides carved with monstrous faces and people and animals leaping around one another. A man winds the handle with one tattooed arm and music pours from the machine's innards.

Michaelis could walk from head to head, he could step on people's voices. Raised hands, beer slants in unsteady glasses, thick white foam rocking over rims. People are all around them, jostling one another, pressing close. Mum touches his foot again, as if she wants to say something, but she still looks straight ahead. Constantine stands alongside. Only the dark hair on the top of his head is visible. It wouldn't matter if he could see Constantine's face. Michaelis never knows how to read it. You know Constantine's mood from what he *does*. Michaelis can feel Dirk's voice through his legs.

'One, two, three!'

The hands of the clock in the cathedral come together. The bell in the tower begins to ring. The canvas arms of the Pepper Shaker lift up towards the sky, over the many windows that glint around its black, cavernous gate. The bell sounds out big brass doles. People are cheering, and Michaelis cheers too. The pipe slips from

17

his mouth into the darkness between people's feet and it is too late now to be careful, too late to catch what has already been dropped.

~

'One time,' Mum says, 'when I got really sick, Constantine found me. I was lying on the ground and I could barely make out the table leg in front of me. My whole body was heavy. I couldn't wake up properly. Your brother shook me; it didn't do any good. I could hear him like it was very far away, but I couldn't answer. Constantine didn't cry. He wasn't scared. He just went next door to Moessie for help. If he hadn't done that, I might never have woken up again at all.'

Moessie is their grandmother. After Mum nearly fell asleep, Constantine lived with Moessie and Michaelis stayed somewhere else. Moessie's clear eyes are buried in the soft wrinkles of her face. They light up when Constantine walks through the door, because she remembers that time when he stayed, which was meant to be short but lasted a year. Mum wasn't allowed to see Constantine then. That was for the best, they said. Now Mum isn't sure. She would hear his voice sometimes from another room when she came by.

'It broke my heart to hear that little voice.'

'Is your heart still broken?'

'No, Michaelis, it's fine now.'

Whenever they visit Moessie, they get a chocolate from a special tin. The wrapping has a gold elephant picture on it, and inside the outer layer of chocolate is a block of caramel that takes a long time to melt. An elephant never forgets. He holds the chocolate in his mouth. A sweet trickle finds its way down the back of his throat while he unfolds and flattens the wrapping, pretending that the elephant is made of real gold. Mum loves elephants. She's always buying statues of them. Everywhere around the house, elephants, made of metal and wood and marble, their trunks lifted.

Mum and Moessie talk in low voices while he is somewhere else in the apartment, away from them, playing with the toys that Moessie keeps in old biscuit tins for the visiting children. *Thunderbirds Are Go.*

Moessie has a small white dog, Baasje. They have the same snowy hair, Moessie and Baasje. The apartment is full of barking and dog smell and squirming movement around their ankles. Moessie pours tea that smells of smoke. It is a mixture of Earl Grey and some other tea that sounds like a Chinese town. Only drink it in good cups. The silver strainer clinks on the cup. The tea pours through and Michaelis sees leaves in slick strands shipwrecked on the metal. The steam rises and finds the windows. Pour the tea first for yourself and last for guests. And for the coffee, you do the opposite.

Moessie's apartment is in a place called the Bunthof. There are two apartment blocks in the Bunthof, thirteen floors high, with a car lot between them. There's also a park and a tree-lined lake alongside that, which often disappears into fog in the morning with only the tops of the trees poking through. It looks like it has been there forever, but people made it all.

'Even the lake?'

'Yes, even the *pond*. Even the fish that live in the water, they don't belong here, those bright orange fish. But they make themselves at home now, don't they?'

'Like Dad?'

'Yes, like Dad.'

Gravity sucks at Michaelis's heart when he takes the elevator to the apartment. Thirteen floors. Watch the light move through the numbers. Constantine knows about gravity. This is why spit falls from the balcony, why people's heads explode when they jump from buildings. It makes Michaelis feel sick as the elevator shudders into motion, and then he forgets that he's moving at all. Until it stops.

Michaelis is in bed at night, with Mum's hand moving through his hair as if it will be there forever.

'I will always love you and Con equally. Don't forget that. I never felt important, not with ten brothers and sisters. I was invisible. And that didn't change until I got sick.'

'How sick did you get, Mum?'

'I got so sick that I could hardly leave the house for two years, not even to play. And my only friend was the teacher who brought me books.'

'Why did you get sick, Mum?'

'It was in my kidneys. I was six, older than you are, but not by much. Your grandmother was about to send me off to school when she noticed the colour of my pee. I had to pee in a bottle for a medical exam at school. The pee was brown, like mud. While she waited for the doctor, she rubbed my neck with balm and wrapped her favourite shawl around it. I don't remember my mother giving me that kind of attention before then, or after. You wouldn't believe how soft that shawl was. Or maybe it is just the thought of it.' Mum's hand stops. 'Time for sleep.'

'Why doesn't Constantine come to bed, too?'

'Because he's three years older. He gets to stay up later. Now go to sleep.'

'I'm not tired.'

'Then pretend.'

Constantine is out there while Michaelis lies in bed alone. He doesn't like his brother, but he feels safer with Con in the room when it is time for sleep. His brother is never afraid.

'Can you leave the door open?'

'A little. But don't make a sound or Dirk will come by and shut it.'

Then he is alone. Whether he is quiet or not, if Dirk finds out the door is open, he will shut it. Michaelis has to learn not to be afraid of the dark, that's why. A narrow rectangle of light plays on his fingers. He pretends that it is alive. He moves the light from one hand to the other. He can hear them in the other room over the noise of the television: Mum on the phone, talking or laughing softly, Dirk sighing or talking to himself or grunting at something on the television. Those sounds never seem to come from the same place at all.

~

Gezellig. This is Mum's word. '*Nou ja, dit is gezellig,*' she says as she shrugs off her coat full of winter rain and puts on a light. *Gezellig.* Indoors you hear it, around talk and tea and coffee and pastries with cinnamon and clove and nutmeg, around Mum's music. You hear it between people, and you cannot touch it because it is a feeling a place has when it is filled with the right kind of things, when it is safe, when Dirk is away.

Michaelis helps around the house when he is too sick for preschool. Sometimes he makes up how sick he feels just to be with her. Mum plays records and makes him a clear soup that has chicken and carrot and small, translucent pieces of cauliflower floating in it.

'After I got sick in my kidneys,' Mum tells him as they sit side by side in the living room folding the washing,

22

'it felt like I was having a very long holiday. The young woman who brought me books would tell me stories just like I do with you. Mostly, though, I'd sit on a day bed in the bay window and watch life go by in the street. There was this man who'd come past on a horsedrawn cart, picking up the rubbish. He'd always give me a smile and leave an apple on the doorstep. I'd hear him come from a long way off, that lonely *clip clop clip clop* down the street. I'd watch my brothers and sisters come home from work and school. There were so many of them, living in this massive attic which had been divided into all of these parts, going off to work, bringing money home for my mother, going out again. But I was the one at home with her. I was the one that needed her. I loved the attention, but I got fat from the medicine the doctors gave me. By the time that I was eight and had to go back to school, I couldn't walk without my legs rubbing together.'

'Really?'

'Really.'

Mum is skinny. You can see the bones in her arms and wrists, the veins like rivers on a map, chasing each other under her pale skin. There is nothing to her at all, except life, the warmth in her voice, the quickness in her large blue eyes. It is hard to imagine her any different.

'Yes, it was a very sad, lonely time after that.'

The washing is done. She's thumbing through her box full of records now as she talks, drawing out each cover for a moment from the wooden box that Dirk made for her. She finally chooses a bright yellow album and turns it slowly between her hands. The Mamas and the Papas.

'I miss London. I bought this the year that your brother was born, when your father and I were still together. We didn't have a lot of money back then, but we were happy. Or I was happy.' She sighs and stares at the record cover without seeing it. 'I've been here too long. It gets claustrophobic, these things that build up around you, that don't let you *be* anything else. It will be good to see something completely different.'

'Clasto...'

'Claustrophobic. Close together. Everything crowding together: memories, people, all the things that they know about you. But we are going somewhere soon that is the opposite of all that. There'll be space. You'll get to fly on a plane.'

'Why?'

'A plane is the easiest way to get there. It's very far away.'

'But why are we going?'

Mum slides the vinyl record from the sleeve and puts it on the player. *California Dreamin'*. She lifts and gently drops the needle into the groove. 'You ask so many questions, Michaelis. Listen. Just listen.'

Australia is an island. You can walk around it and never get off the beach. The beach is tropical. That's why they are going, because the beaches are lovely. He knows only the beach here in Holland with its damp, clinging sand and icy water and the hot chips in a conical paper bag heaped with finely chopped onions and mayonnaise. But you have to drive forever to get to this beach, and when you're there, you know you'll have to go back, with all the other cars crowded on the flat, endless road. Everyone in Holland wants to make the most of summer's hot days.

'We'll be there before you know it,' Mum says.

It never feels that way. They move so slowly, with all the traffic, that you can count birds in the trees. Michaelis has been to the beach twice that he can remember. He can count to twenty, and after that things get confused. After that he can throw out numbers, but he gets the order all wrong.

2

Now Mum has to go and he has to stay.

'You'll be fine. Really. *Echt waar.*'

Words from home, but suddenly they are out of place. Home is too far away to imagine. Dad, Moessie, the Bunthof, Bergen op Zoom—they are memories now. They went to Amsterdam and boarded the plane and there was nothing to see through the windows except clouds and blue sky and night. The whine of engines was constant and everything stretched and stretched.

The plane took them to a place called Sydney. For a few weeks, they lived in a warren of rooms with other people from other countries. Dirk and Mum talked about where to go next. They looked at maps and said the names of strange cities out loud and traced journeys with their fingers. Constantine kept to himself.

'Leave him alone,' Mum told Dirk. 'He's upset.'

For Michaelis there was only waiting—no more going to preschool, no more games, just waiting. Then they bought an old car and drove along a winding road through bushland with occasional glimpses of the sea. They headed to a place called Newcastle.

'Come on,' Mum says.

Michaelis clings to Mum's leg and he can't bring himself to look in at the noise and the movement of the classroom behind him. A woman unpeels his arms and traps him in an embrace. The door opens and shuts. Mum is on the other side of the closed door, walking away. He can hear her steps, rapid and jerky, full of unhappiness. He can't smell her perfume anymore. The woman talks at him. He can't understand a word she is saying except now, now, now.

He struggles, she holds on, her arms tensing, one bony wrist close to his mouth. Children are laughing behind him. He bites down on the wrist, writhes in the slackening of her grip, kicks her shin, and makes a break for the desks stacked against the end of the room. The carpet burns his knees as he crawls to the dark corner. He sits there against the wall.

The life of the classroom goes on. The teacher talks to the other children and they calm down. They glance sometimes in his direction, under the table, but they are kept busy by the teacher's voice. He sees mainly their legs, skinny and bare, because it's summer and it's unbearably hot.

The ceiling fan turns in slow, wobbling circles like a wheel about to come off. The scrawled paintings tacked to the wall flutter towards the open window. A swollen fly skids and bounces against the glass above the opening. The children have forgotten about him. They look the same in their grey uniforms, just two different kinds— boys and girls. The girls have white socks, the boys have grey with two thin gold lines, bunched down around shiny black shoes.

The teacher crouches down and their eyes meet. Michaelis is too far away for her to reach him. She smiles tightly, and her forehead notches into an impatient frown. She speaks again, in the same tone that she used before. Michaelis stares back over his tucked-up knees. She disappears.

'How was your first day at school?'

Michaelis doesn't answer. Mum asks again, and when he stays quiet, she sighs and walks ahead. The moment stretches out. His rage dulls. He has set it in motion, this silence between them, but he can't break it. He wants to say that it's okay, that he's happy again now that they are together, he wants to tell her how bad it all was in this strange place where all of his words are useless. But he can't open his mouth. He speeds up his stride to match hers, and stares at the cracks in the concrete path. School is behind him, yet ahead too, always ahead. He wishes that he could forget about that. Looking ahead is the worst part.

Each morning, Mum walks him up the gloomy street beneath the arch of branches, towards the school, avoiding dips and rises in the footpath where the roots are coming through. The trees make the sunlight lazy and broken. Don't talk on the way up. The road is impossibly steep. Look straight ahead, to the end of the road, and you can see only blue sky. As if you might walk straight into it.

The teacher's name is Mrs K. Michaelis is starting to understand some of the things she says, but not enough to make it worth listening.

His seat is at the back of the class. His gaze drifts to the window and the huge sky beyond it, the tall, wasted trees with their thin leaves. Red leaves and scrolls of bark fall with each hot gust of wind. The leaves crack into a thousand pieces when you crush them in your palm. The air is so dry that it hurts your lungs. It hasn't rained for weeks. Back home, it's always raining. People sit inside, smoking and eating and talking about the rain. *Gezellig*. The sky back home is so low that you can scoop water out of the clouds with your hand.

The classroom has gone quiet, but he doesn't realise until it's too late. Mrs K has come up behind him. She flicks his ear with her ruler, short and sharp like a bee sting, and walks off.

'Pay attention,' she says.

These are the only words she says slowly. The other children stop giggling and turn back to the front. They screw up their faces and lean over their books. Michaelis doesn't do this. He knows that all *he* has to do is follow Mrs K with his eyes.

At the end of the day, Mrs K lets the children touch her belly. 'There is a baby inside me. Feel.'

The children line up in front of her, each taking their turn. Her bare stomach is round and taut. The belly button is a knot straining at the middle.

'Go on, touch me.' She holds up her blouse and smiles, as if that is all it takes to be kind, to have a child inside you.

The next day, Mrs K tells the children to open their books. They will practise writing the letter *f*. Except for Michaelis. A boy stands at the door with a note.

'Go with him,' Mrs K says.

In an empty classroom, a man sits behind a kid's desk. He is hunched over in a suit, playing with puzzles. He smiles when he catches sight of Michaelis. He takes off his jacket and rolls up his sleeves.

'Do you want to play, too? Can you help me with this puzzle?'

Without talking, they work it out together. When it's done, they start a new one.

'Do you know why you're here?'

Michaelis shrugs.

'How old are you?'

'Five.'

'Do you like school?'

Michaelis shrugs again.

The man nods as if that was the right answer. 'Where are you from?'

'Holland.'

'What's Holland like? Take your time.'

As he works on the puzzle, Michaelis begins talking. Words from home tumble into his sentences. He talks about Dad and football in the park. He tells the man about the endless rain—*de regen*—about his ten uncles and aunts, one for each finger, though he never saw most of them, and about snowy-haired Moessie who lives with a white dog, Baasje, on the top floor of an apartment block called the Bunthof. Underneath the apartment block stretches a dimly lit tunnel with lots of doors. Each door leads to a dry, stale-smelling room like a prison cell, except people put bikes and old stuff they don't need down there. Moessie is always shoving stuff out of sight; Mum said that about her once.

Michaelis runs out of words and has to draw pictures.

'You're a good drawer.'

'I am born dere.' Michaelis points to the top of the apartment block.

He has heard the story so many times that it is as if he remembers for himself. The midwife with a cigarette in her mouth. Dad turning up late and having to borrow money for flowers.

'Very good,' the man says. 'You have lots of windmills in Holland, don't you? Want to build one together?'

They mix water and flour and it turns into glue. The man shows him how to curl a piece of white paper into a cone and cut around the bottom so that it can stand on its base. Michaelis tells the man about a windmill near where he used to live. It had windows and pots out the front overflowing with yellow and red flowers in spring. People lived in it. Or maybe this is a story that someone told him or maybe it was a picture. Some things become strange when you say them out loud. Dad chasing them around the house in his pyjamas. *Animaaales*. The man helps him put the vanes on the windmill with a thumbtack, and they blow against them from the side. The vanes don't turn very well.

The man laughs. 'The idea is always better when it stays in your head.'

After that, they play some more puzzles. They race each other.

'You're faster than me, clever boy.' The man ruffles Michaelis's hair. 'You'll be fine.'

But Michaelis knows the man is letting him win.

~

'This is how I met Dirk.'

Mum stirs a pot of macaroni and milk and sultanas spiced with cinnamon and nutmeg and clove. They will eat the pudding after dinner, and the rest will go in the fridge. Mum will cut it into cold, slimy squares, Michaelis will take it to the school, and other kids will pause nearby and glance down at him with looks of curiosity and distaste. They eat different things here: pasties, meat pies, sponge squares covered in chocolate and shredded coconut.

'It was a dark time in my life,' Mum says as she circles the spoon around the edge of the pot, 'after your father, after what happened to me. My family didn't want much to do with me. Dirk came up to me in a bar. He seemed so solid. He told me that we had something in common, that we both needed a good shave.' Mum laughs. 'He was never good with people. But he was kind to me. For a while, he was very kind to me. Anyway, out of the frying pan, into the fire.'

'What does that mean?'

'Nothing. It means that when you make one mistake, it's easier to make another.' She gives a slight shake of her head, then looks across at him and smiles. 'No. It doesn't really mean anything. I'm just talking.'

Dirk lies on his back on the shore. Waves foam and draw back around his feet. His belly hugs his sides. The colour has drained from his face, but his beard holds a golden film of sand. Hair plasters his chest in black clumps like seaweed. The man bending over Dirk is tanned and wiry and a lot shorter. It's hard to imagine that he just dragged Dirk out of the water.

'All right, mate?'

Dirk gets to his feet, sways, and thuds back down.

The man puts a hand on his shoulder. 'Sit back, mate. Sit back. Take a deep breath. Just stay between the flags next time, mate. That's what they're there for, the flags. Strong rip this arvo.'

The nearest flag cracks and straightens out again on the breeze. *Rip*. Michaelis searches the water, but he can't see anything. He doesn't even know what he should be looking for.

'We're going,' Dirk says. 'Get Con.'

Constantine has already worked out how to catch waves across the shoreline. He tucks himself inside the glassy barrels of water that break on the sand. There are a few other boys there alongside him, but none manage it the way he does. Michaelis shouts to him. His brother turns and stares straight through him. Michaelis keeps waving his arms. The water shapes before him into a wave and sucks the sand from beneath his feet. He falls and kicks against nothing. The next wave throws him back. He splutters with a mouthful of foam.

Constantine emerges alongside, dark hair flat against his forehead. He's holding a jellyfish. With a grin, he drops it onto Michaelis's belly and jogs past.

~

'He wasn't listening,' Dirk says. '*Verdomme*. I told him three times. All I did was give him a tap on the back of the head.'

'You hurt him. Everyone was looking.'

'Maybe you should spend a bit more time thinking about *me*.'

'Don't be jealous.'

'I'm not jealous, *verdomme*. He just has to carry on and you go running to him, pandering to every weakness.'

'Michaelis is a little boy and you're a man.'

'*Verdomme. Godverdomme.*'

'What's wrong now?'

'The car. It's stuck.'

The engine groans and revs into the stillness, the car shudders and does not move. The smell of the clutch drifts around them. They get out of the car. The sun bleeds over the dunes. Mosquitoes waft in lazy swarms through the beams of the headlights. A wall of saltbush grows larger either side. In the stillness, you can hear the roar of the sea. It is not yet night, but getting darker all the time. The soft yellow sand gathered around the tyres is growing dim.

Dirk slaps his neck and stares at Mum. 'Get in, turn the engine, and I'll push. You boys help. Push when I say.'

Mum gets in the car.

'Now!'

The ignition scrapes into life and dies again.

'No, *verdomme*. I said now! Are you even listening? For God's sake! It's simple!'

'I can't drive, Dirk!'

'*Idioot!* Push! Pay attention!'

It is pitch black by the time they stop trying.

'We're just getting deeper into the sand,' Dirk says. 'Turn off the lights. Wait in the car. I'll go and get help.'

'How long will that take?'

'I don't know.'

Mum crosses her arms and turns away from him. 'All of these beaches in Newcastle, and you wanted to drive for forty-five minutes to the only one without a proper road. Well, go then.'

They sit, the three of them together in the darkness of the car, with the night and the light of a large moon pressing against the windows. Con is tapping on the door of the car.

Mum keeps her arms against her chest. 'It's horrible, that darkness. Anyone could be out there.'

Con shifts in his seat and leans forward. 'This reminds me of a story I heard...'

Mum gives a short, dissatisfied sigh. 'Don't start, Con. Just don't start. I don't need you making things worse.'

'Okay then.'

Mum begins sobbing. Her shoulders shake. 'I don't know. I just don't know.'

'What, Mum?'

'I don't know why we came here. What was I thinking?'

Constantine and Michaelis watch her in silence. Her whole body shudders with her sobs. Michaelis thinks and tries to understand. Every now and again, Mum flicks on the lights of the car, as if to remind herself of something. As she does, Michaelis sees all the insect life swirling against the shadowy backdrop of dunes, on and off, on and off, the life revealed for a moment before disappearing again.

3

Walk in any direction and you'll soon come across lawns, roads, footpaths and weatherboard houses. But, as Michaelis stares into the tangle of shadows and trees, he finds this easy to forget. Bat urine fills the air, cockatoos screech overhead in metallic calls. Kangaroos and wallabies slouch and hop on the other side of a wire fence. Further along, a pair of wedge-tailed eagles hunch inside their wings in a concrete cage. There are barbecues everywhere, ancient stone-and-brick squares with fire-darkened hot plates, scattered along the tracks, circles of stones holding small mountains of chopped wood. Between them, people playing cricket, kicking balls, laughing, talking, holding beers.

'You couldn't imagine it back home,' Mum says. 'This heat.'

She still talks about home as though they might turn the car around and go there. Michaelis thinks suddenly of *Carnaval*, the crowded marketplace, all cobbled and hard underfoot, stone surfaces and dark windows rising everywhere around them, throwing back and mixing the people's voices.

'*Verdomme.*' Dirk flicks his hand at the mosquitoes that float in over the open window and come to rest on cheeks and necks. '*Verdomme.* Everywhere you go, these damn mosquitoes.'

There is a fleck of white paint on his ear. Dirk is helping to build a police station in the city. They went to see it yesterday. The station is a grey bunker complex overlooking the ocean. It looks like something under siege. Dirk comes home every day from work covered in paint and glue and dust. He speaks mainly in English but swears in Dutch.

'*Daar,*' Mum says. 'There.'

They pull over and get out their things. Dirk pours beer over the barbecue plate and scrapes away layers of grime. He is always hitching his belt up under his belly. The sausages and the onions burn and they've forgotten the tomato sauce again. Mum takes one bite of a sausage and puts her plate to the side.

Constantine's friend James has come along with them. After the barbecue, Michaelis wanders behind them, listening in to their conversation about vampires and werewolves, although he knows that it will give him nightmares. Constantine suddenly looks back over his shoulder. In that instant, he becomes Dad, with his brilliant hazelnut eyes and the gleam of his perfect teeth.

'Go away.'

Michaelis stares at him.

'Go away. Out of here. *Fuck off.*'

Michaelis wanders off alone. He hasn't heard much about him, but now Dad is there again, at the heart of his thoughts. Maybe he was always there, because Michaelis remembers him easily, his aftershave, the roughness of his cheek, and it feels as if he has been missing him forever. As if that might be the source of the sadness that comes to him in quiet moments when he is lying in bed or playing alone. Dad is no longer part of their lives. Mum will only say Dad's name on the phone to Moessie and to her sister. Andreas, Andreas, Andreas. This is Dad's other name. Repeat it under your breath as you walk along in the afternoon sun, and see if the meaning changes.

He comes across an ant heap. The ants are big and orange and stalk across the dry sand in busy, complicated patterns. He squats down between them and watches. The ants are searching for something. They meet one another, confer, keep searching. One ant is dragging another back to the mouth of the heap. It stops every now and again, then picks up the other ant and keeps moving. The other ant does not move. It is bent inwards and has a leg missing. The two of them make a mysterious pair. Are they friends, he wonders, or will one eat the other?

'Micha-ayleees!'

The voice is friendly, warm. He lifts his head. Something fills his head with a *thwock*. There is pain and everything blackens. Rocks and twigs dig into his back. He feels sick. Someone is crying. He wants to throw up.

There is water on his eye. The sky is spinning itself out of fog.

'Are you okay? Are you okay?' Mum lifts him to his feet and touches his face. Her hand comes away covered in blood. Constantine is on the other side of her, James standing behind him with a fascinated half-smile.

'I didn't mean to hit him. It was a joke.'

Constantine is talking to Dirk, but Dirk doesn't say anything at all. He lifts Con by the hair and kicks him towards the car. People watch briefly before turning back to their barbecues. Constantine never cries or moves at times like this. He goes silent, a focused, empty look on his face, like a boy competing in some sport.

~

'A dog will make it feel more like home, don't you think?'

Michaelis touches the scar above his eye and thinks of Moessie's dog back in Holland. He glances up at Mum, the blush and the blue eye shadow she has put on her face, the paleness of her skin underneath. She meets his gaze and he nods and smiles.

They have already lived in a handful of houses and neighbourhoods, but she fills each place with the vinyl crackle of her records from Holland, the smell of her cooking, and her perfume that lingers from one room to another. Patchouli. If the carpet is old, she buys a

41

covering made from straw tiles and lays it everywhere so that a fresh smell fills the house. On damp nights, you smell the carpet underneath anyway.

'Here,' the man says, handing a leash over to Dirk. A black labrador with a gleaming coat strains against the other end.

'Barry will be fine,' the man says, scratching his ribs under his blue singlet. 'Yeah. He'll be right when I go.'

Barry whimpers. Constantine stands nearby, peeling bark from a stick. The man gets into his ute and drives off.

'There,' Mum says, 'now we have a dog for the backyard.'

Constantine gives the stick an impatient wave. 'Can I take him to the park now?'

Dirk closes the gate and unclips the leash from Barry's collar. The dog explodes from his grasp, bolts to the end of the yard, around the clothes hoist, and back past them.

'Barry!' Con waves the stick.

Barry clears the wire gate with a leap, skids on the tar and keeps running. They walk out onto the street. Barry swerves around a car at the intersection, flinches at a horn and disappears on the other side. Dirk scratches his neck.

Mum is holding her throat. 'Goodness. Do you think he'll come back? Should we go after him?'

'*Verdomme.* Can you even see him anymore?'

'Well, I guess we can wait and see. Maybe he'll come back. It's not that I don't understand how he feels.'

'What?'

'Nothing. It's nothing.'

They stand there for a while longer. Mum and Dirk go inside. Constantine uses his stick to hit a tennis ball against a wall. Again and again, rarely missing, the ball echoing against the bricks until Dirk comes outside and tells him to stop or else.

The road is soft with heat in the summer, the tar surface treacly and bubbling around the edges. Sometimes he picks loose, soft bits and shapes them with a stick. It reminds him of something Mum said, about growing up in Holland, an explosion in a neighbourhood liquorice factory. And how they ate the chunks of smoky liquorice that fell like soft hail around the nearby streets.

Michaelis is walking towards the house of his new friend, Nikki, a pale, freckled boy with blond hair and a gentle manner. Nikki's house is hidden from the world by a tall green fence, on the corner of the next street. Michaelis is almost six and Mum lets him go there alone.

As he walks to Nikki's place, Michaelis feels some sort of strange tension drain out of him. Most of the time, he is not even aware of the tension until he leaves the house. Lizards scurry away from his feet into the crisp, dry leaves in the gutters.

Nikki's backyard has a mulberry tree. There are mulberry trees everywhere—in people's gardens, in the overgrown places between the houses or at the edges of parks—and they give up their smell at night along with the frangipani trees and jasmine bushes. Springy bows crowded with hand-sized leaves and swollen mulberries sway over Nikki's fence and drape towards the footpath.

When Michaelis pauses to pluck a handful, his gaze drifts across the intersection to his new school under a brooding canopy of fig and eucalyptus trees. Hamilton South. Owls and bats sleep in the trees. They are quiet during the day, but you hear them stirring as the sun drops down. Clouds of birds gather from the fiery summer sky, screaming over one another, hidden from the world, as if it is the trees themselves coming to life.

Michaelis can hear the hum of the pool filter. He has to lean on his toes to hook his arm through the hole in Nikki's fence. He scrapes his arm against metal until he finds the catch, and swings in on his toes with the gate.

The pool in the backyard is deep and clear as a tropical lagoon. Michaelis and Nikki fight together on inflatable pool ponies. They swim until they are shivering, then lie on the warm stone path side by side, talking, daydreaming, the water evaporating from their backs.

When they tire of the pool and the sunlight, they wander into the house. They play on a machine called an Atari. It connects to the television with a cord and you play games using a joystick. Nikki lets him choose the games. Moonsweeper. Tank Battle. Space Invaders. A spaceship made of white pixels glides from side to side on the gleaming, bulbous curve of the screen. Michaelis controls it and pretends the fate of the world rests on his shoulders. Nikki watches his tense, earnest expression and can't stop laughing. Some laughter makes Michaelis blush. Not Nikki's.

After the Atari, Nikki's father comes in and puts on a movie for them. One wall of the living room is a bookshelf. It's not full of books but videotapes, the titles typed onto small white labels. Nikki's father watches movies and says if they are any good. That's his job. With Nikki, Michaelis has seen *The Wizard of Oz* more times than he can count. And he has seen *The Elephant Man*, which made him cry, and all of the *Star Wars* movies over and over again. The video machine is a mystery to him. Like the Atari, he didn't even know such a thing existed until he met Nikki.

The mess in every room of Nikki's house is at odds with the way in which Mum keeps things at home. It's hard to walk around without stepping on something from the *Star Wars* galaxy. Nikki owns a large cardboard model of the Death Star, the ice station of Hoth, a handful of intricately designed spaceships. They play with them together for hours, inventing all sorts of scenarios. Nikki has too many toys to keep track of. He gave Michaelis a stormtrooper once, all white and fresh out of the packet. Mum made Michaelis give it right back.

'One day you'll understand,' she said.

This is what happened when he got a present from Dad's relatives. They have relatives somewhere near

Newcastle, from the Greek–Cypriot side. Mum couldn't believe it when she found out, but when you are Greek you find relatives everywhere, or they find you. Dad sent money all the way from Holland, and a short, fat woman—Dad's sister—turned up and gave Constantine and Michaelis presents. Constantine got the official soccer ball from the last World Cup and Michaelis got a plastic aeroplane.

Constantine is the firstborn and he should get more according to the Greeks. Not according to Mum. And even though Michaelis was happy with his aeroplane, Mum took both presents and gave them back.

'Either you spend the same money on both of them,' she told the woman, 'or you don't give them anything at all.'

When Mum says these things, there is never any doubt in her voice. The woman looked at Mum like she was crazy and they never heard from her again. Later, Mum said that Michaelis was mistaken, that it wasn't about the presents at all, but that when she'd talked to them about Dad, they hadn't liked what they heard.

One of the movies that Nikki's father puts on for them is black and white. A man invents a machine that makes things smaller and accidentally shrinks himself. The man grows backwards. He becomes as small as a boy, then smaller. He tries to figure out how to stop shrinking. A cat chases him into a doll's house. He fights a spider

46

with a toothpick. In the last part of the movie, he keeps shrinking, smaller than a speck of dust, smaller, smaller. Smaller. The man wonders what will happen when he shrinks into nothingness. That's how the movie ends.

Afterwards, Michaelis can't stop thinking about it. He often has this dream about running along a wide, empty road. At the end of the road there's a square pit and it's full of spiders with legs longer than his body. He's running so fast that he can't stop. He's terrified of the spiders but for some reason, with a strange, horrible enthusiasm, he jumps right in. That's always the moment he wakes up.

'After you die, you go to this place where you live forever,' Nikki says quietly as he angles the *Millennium Falcon* along his bedroom walls, Han Solo rattling inside the cockpit. 'It's called the afterlife.'

Michaelis can't imagine anything more frightening than living forever. When he gets home, he asks Mum about the afterlife.

'Of course there's an afterlife,' she says. 'I made a deal with your grandfather once. Whoever died first would come back to let the other know. One night, my father was sitting in his favourite chair. He was in the middle of one of his stories. He lifted one finger, opened his mouth to say something, and died. Something happened in his brain. Just like that. It was very peaceful. A few months later, when I was staying at your grandmother's, I woke up to find my father standing over me. He was dressed in his favourite suit. He smiled. I blinked and he was gone.'

As Michaelis listens, he pictures Moessie's apartment, a place full of old, heavy furniture that you could never imagine moving, the place where he was born, where his grandfather once lived and slipped from the edge of the world. There is a massive painting of two fish in a fishbowl. The ornate gold picture frame looks like it would kill you if it fell on you. Oil colours are layered on the surface. The painting seems covered in dust, but isn't.

One fish is black, the other orange. They're floating side by side in the bowl. The black fish has eyes the size of apples. Next to the painting is a figure carved into wood, a halo over his head. It's Jesus. He's smiling and he's making the okay sign. When it's quiet, you hear the grandfather clock. It has a window in the cabinet and a brass disc swings inside the glass. Time goes forwards, memories fall backwards. Every now and again, in the house of his grandparents, the clock booms and the sound swells through the house, and you feel it in the air long after it's finished, like the beat of a brass heart.

~

The midday sun hurts his eyes. A teacher runs towards the sick bay, and Michaelis only glimpses what she carries: a boy slumped in her arms. A boy covered in blood.

The boy is howling, and Michaelis didn't see his face.

Someone grabs his shoulder. Carl. 'He's hurt really bad. Let's go.'

Michaelis lets Carl guide him along. They hear wailing from the sick bay. A teacher tells them to go away. The voice sounds all raw echoing in the corridor, more like an animal than a boy.

Michaelis still isn't sure if the boy is Con. He follows Carl to the toilets. The toilets are wet and dark and smell of urine. The tiles are slick with it. Sometimes boys hide and shoot piss at the younger kids as they walk inside.

Carl hunches over the taps and scrubs his face with water. He has a big, round face like the moon, his hair like windblown grass piled on the top of it. He paces from one side of the toilets to the other. Michaelis realises that he's crying.

'He's my best mate. His head is split right open. I was chasing him, so it was my fault. We were playing tips. I'll never forgive myself if he dies. My dad died, you know. Brain cancer. I don't want to lose my best mate, too.'

Michaelis doesn't know what to say. People always seem so devoted to his brother.

Carl stops sobbing and ruffles Michaelis's hair. 'He'll be all right, Mike. I'll look out for you if he's not.'

These words make him worry. Sometimes he hates his brother and wishes him dead, but he also has dreams in which his brother actually gets killed and he wakes up crying. And he'll glance at the bottom bunk and see his brother asleep and feel a tender sense of relief. It never lasts long.

'Serves you right,' Dirk says at the dinner table that night, 'for being an idiot.'

He glares at Constantine, daring him to say any different. Con fingers the wound and the three stitches that pull it together.

'Don't touch it,' Mum says with a shake of her head. 'You're always getting hurt. I'll bet you were showing off. Reminds me of when you were little, back home. That time when you were hanging upside down on the monkey bars by your legs. Well, that girl showed you.'

'What happened, Mum?'

Michaelis knows. He just wants to hear the story again.

'The little girl took both his feet and flipped them off the bar. He cried all the way home. Even after I bought him an ice-cream, he kept on with it, so I knew he was serious. Turns out he'd broken his arm.'

'And what about the time he pretended to go to school?'

Mum laughs and even Dirk is smiling now, his heavy jaw squared off inside his beard.

'Oh, yes!' Mum says. 'When I used to drop him at kindergarten and he'd always refuse to walk through the door until I was gone. He'd just stand there staring back at me until I went away. One afternoon, after school, we went shopping together, and this little girl walked over and asked him why he hadn't been at school. Turns out that he used to go to the park across from the school after I left. He'd spend the day playing by himself and arrive at the school gates when it was time to be picked up.

He'd tell me all of these stories about what he'd been doing at school, but it was all made up.' Mum leans across and strokes Constantine's hair, a relaxed, faraway look on her face. 'He was always good at keeping secrets.'

~

'The leadlight windows are beautiful, don't you think, boys?' Mum hugs Michaelis and Constantine close and gives a determined nod. 'Everyone will want to live in Carrington soon. You'll see. All of these houses will get done up and it will be such a pretty street. We're getting in early.'

They are standing in front of their latest house, an old miner's cottage wedged between other cottages. Dirk takes his pipe from his mouth and taps the ash out against his pants. 'It doesn't need too much work. Paint. Rip up the carpet. Sand and polish the boards.'

He's not really talking to anyone, only himself. He begins stuffing the pipe with more tobacco. There are lines of grease and dirt along his fingers and under his nails. He sometimes sits on the couch and uses a nail file to scrape the undersides of his nails clean. When he does this, with his feet flung out before him, his forehead mounts over his eyes and he looks like a child left waiting too long for his parents.

Their street is wide enough for teams of oxen to turn around with their loads of coal, except there aren't any oxen here anymore. The miners have long since moved on, too. The coal is still nearby, though, heaped up in mountains at the next suburb along, waiting to be loaded onto ships. The dust from the coal is on the fence when you run your finger across it.

At one end of the broad road, there is saltbush. Beyond the bushes, the ground loses itself in mounds of dirt and rubble. Past that is the restless expanse of the harbour, seeping and receding through a mess of mangroves near the shore, roots littered with plastic bags, bottles, syringes, fragments of pornographic magazines, a mattress, the murky water lapping from this to the decaying old warehouses on the other side.

'And you can walk to school,' Mum says.

Through waves of heat, Michaelis can make out the latest school and he has seen it up close already: a stretch of asphalt hemmed in by a wire fence, brick buildings with drab paint peeling from the window frames and the doors, all of it full of menace even when it's empty. Weathered steel monkey bars, graffiti over the bike shed and toilets, the stall of bubblers, half with twigs stuffed into the holes. The grass on the fields looks dead, all burnt at the tips and faded, straggling in clumps from the dusty earth.

'Yes,' Dirk says. 'It's a good place to buy in.'

Mum gives another quick, tight nod. 'And there's a backyard for Harmony.'

Dirk brought Harmony back to Alexander Street one day. He got her from someone at work. He pulled up in the station wagon, opened the door, and Harmony came out, slapping her tail like she was coming home, as if she'd been doing it all her life.

'She's a hunting breed,' he told the boys, 'but she doesn't have the killing instinct.'

Plenty of people here do, though. Mr Smith, the principal of the new school, has a compact body inside a brown suit, penetrating black eyes, a pencil moustache and salt-and-pepper hair combed sparsely across his shiny skull. On the wall behind him, the school motto is emblazoned in gold on a wooden plaque. *Honour above all*. Mr Smith rises from behind his desk and shakes Mum's hand. He looks at the boys.

When he speaks, he clips off each word. 'Welcome to Carrington Public, boys. I'll show you something interesting.' He opens a glass cabinet and pulls out a cane. It slices through the air. 'This is for when you transgress.'

Michaelis feels his hand tighten into Mum's.

When you get caned, you hold out your hand. Count your age—that's how many blows you'll get across the palm. Call every teacher *Mr* or *Mrs* or *Sir*, and the men will call you *son*, as if they are all your fathers.

At home, it is no different.

'Put it in your mouth,' Dirk says.

The liver sits on his fork, a slippery piece of illness.

He slides it onto his tongue, brings his teeth together. Something rises at the back of his throat.

Dirk lifts one hand. 'Don't you dare.'

Mum's plaintive voice breaks in. 'He doesn't *have* to eat it.'

'You cooked it. He eats it.' He turns back to Michaelis. 'If you vomit, I'll still make you eat it.'

Michaelis tries to swallow. Bile swells his cheeks, making him want to vomit even more, and then he does, a little, into his mouth. Dirk leans towards him, the hand still raised, the wedding ring glinting over a dirt-grained knuckle.

'*Wil je een klap?* Swallow.'

Klap. The sound the hand makes when it lands flat, close to your ear. Michaelis swallows. Dirk's mouth pulls down at the corners. He studies Michaelis.

'Do it again,' he says in a low voice. 'This time chew properly.'

When Dirk drops them off at the cinema to watch *E.T.*, Constantine sneaks Michaelis into *Conan the Barbarian* instead. It's rated R. It's meant to be for adults. Michaelis has never seen anything so full of blood and violence.

At the start of the movie, when Conan is a boy, his tribe is massacred and he is enslaved. He grows into a man by pushing around an enormous wooden wheel. That's how he spends the rest of his childhood: alone, chained to a wheel, walking around and around in circles, until he grows lean and strong. And then he escapes and goes on a quest to find the man who killed his parents. Michaelis loves the bare-breasted women and cannot look away from the blood and beheadings.

'Who is your father, if it is not me?' the villain asks Conan at the end. 'Who gave you the will to live?'

Michaelis doesn't know. Constantine's eyes shine in the darkness beside him. Con is nine, three years older than him. They are sitting right at the front, below the screen, their heads craning. Above them, with all his gleaming muscles knotted pensively, Conan the Barbarian looks like he wants to say something thoughtful, like he might even want to agree with the villain, but instead he cuts off the man's head and throws it down a set of stone stairs. Now that's a way to answer a question. The head thuds down each step and rolls away. Then Conan sets the villain's temple on fire. Each time light blazes from the screen, it washes across Con's face and reveals it, like something carved from stone.

Michaelis should be used to getting hit, should be getting toughened up himself. But the only time a teacher tries to take him off to be caned, he collapses and has to be dragged along. His shirt tears at the sleeve. He shrieks and sobs. Others are watching; Michaelis doesn't care.

'Oh, for God's sake,' the teacher says. 'Be a *man* about it!'

Michaelis makes himself a dead weight on the ground. The teacher gives up in disgust and walks off. Michaelis picks himself up. He has lost the opportunity to be a man about it, to be like Conan the Barbarian. He wipes his hands on his shorts, feeling the eyes of other kids on the hot surface of his face.

If he had to do it all over again, he would do the same.

All he wants to do is get home. But as he leaves the classroom, with his head hunched into his collar, he hears the news from kids running past. Some boy called Tom, huge and drunk and twelve years old, wants to beat up Con. Michaelis runs after the other children, but by the time he gets there, people are walking away.

Tom is sitting on the ground holding his nose, stunned by the blood running down his wrists. Constantine, bag slung over his back, kicks at an old can as he walks down the street. He's whistling out of the corner of his mouth, like a gunslinger. Michaelis follows at a distance.

They go home and take Harmony to the park. There's no one else around. A hot, dry wind blows from the direction of the factories on the other side of the harbour. The horizon is tinged yellow. A thick, sulphurous tang saturates the air. You can see cracks in the ground and green ants scuttling across it through the brown-edged grass. Blue silos to one side, the bridge on the other. Vapour ripples up from the road that runs towards the bridge.

At night, the walls of their house dissolve into the summer humidity and clanging noise of the harbour. You can hear the clamour, as if the container ships are gliding past the house, sending out their booming greetings and farewells straight into the bedroom.

Squinting against the sun now, Constantine throws a stick with a smooth, effortless motion, and it looks like it might disappear into the sky. Harmony brings it back and gazes up at him, down on her haunches, ready to spring into motion. She likes playing fetch. She'll do it endlessly—just don't ask her to *kill* the stick.

Mum said they should get Harmony desexed, but they don't have the money. Later she says it was a big mistake. She says it on a really hot evening while she's peeling potatoes over the sink. The cloudy sky through the window is on fire. The sun has disappeared, but heat rises through the floorboards and sweat sits on your skin. Tiny dust shapes spin in the sunlight. Outside, there's another dog scrabbling at the fence, and Harmony's howling at the end of her chain.

'For God's sake,' Mum says. 'She's in heat.'

She holds her belly and sighs, and there's a look in her eyes as if she might burst into tears.

4

Jonno doesn't weigh a thing. Michaelis holds his new brother and grins at the camera. Dirk takes the picture, his mouth heavy inside the beard.

'I can't believe you're letting him do that.'

'He'll be all right.' Mum stands beside Michaelis, hands planted above her hips, palms pressing into her lower back, as if she still has the weight inside her. The air is drowsy with bees and smells of honey from the bushes crowded with white and yellow daisies. Michaelis is six, but in a few months he will be seven. He can stick his tongue between his front teeth. He wishes that they were straight like Con's.

'Your teeth are fine,' Mum says. 'You don't want to look perfect.'

He sees Mum sometimes, from the edge of the school-yard, where he plays alone with a view all the way down to his house. She walks along the street, arms crossed,

staring ahead. Jonno isn't with her. She looks like she is
going somewhere, but then she returns, with a look like
she can't remember why she started out in the first place.

For a while, after school, he starts taking twenty-cent
coins from Mum's wallet and buying assorted lollies at
the corner store: cobbers, milk bottles, freckles, white-
chocolate buttons. The idea came from Constantine, and
it's an adventure until Dirk catches him at it, picks him
up by the hair, carries him into his room, and hits him
until long after he has promised never to do it again.

But in the late afternoons, he still steals a box of
matches when he can from Dirk's supply and crouches in
the gutter near the mangroves in the harbour at the end
of the street. He works his way through the matches, one
at a time, striking them, watching the flame burn towards
his thumb, and he thinks of being inside a stranded
car, surrounded by the wilderness, Mum flicking the
headlights on and off, looking for what?

And then, a few months after Jonno's birth, Dirk and
Mum pack the car for a long trip. Harmony does not
come along.

'Where would we fit her?' Mum asks them.

It's true. The back of the station wagon is full of their
things and that's where Harmony usually goes.

'Where are we going?'

'You'll see.'

They drive with Jonno in the back, between Michaelis and Constantine.

'How far away is it?'

'You'll know when we get there.'

They eat McDonald's and stay in a hotel where you can hear traffic on the highway all night, and drive again the next day. They stop at service stations and for a while at a beach with pale sand that slopes beneath the clear blue water forever. Holding Jonno, Mum walks into the water in her dress, which floats white and luminescent up around her calves. They get back into the car. Michaelis sleeps.

Mum shifts suddenly in the front seat and looks back at them. 'We're here.'

The sun is gone. A long, broad bridge stretches under a summer evening sky over an expanse of water beyond which he can see a darkening shoreline crowded with saltbush.

'There, on the other side, that's where we'll live now.'

Everything on Bribie Island broods. The long, straight roads boil with heat. Tar and sand scald and toughen the soles of Michaelis's feet. The brown, leathery corpses of toads sit on the roads baking in the sun, dried blood around them. You can see storms coming in from the sea. The water is flat. There are waves on the other side of the island, but you forget that they even exist. Like your father. Blue-grey clouds spill into the horizon and tighten with convulsions of light and throbbing booms of thunder.

He goes swimming with Con in the outlet to a lagoon that pokes like a finger from the ocean into the land. A tree, stripped of bark and leaves, leans over the water and they jump from one of its dead branches.

All day the tide moves in that place, carrying out the silty waters of the mangrove swamp or bringing in currents from the flat sea. They climb up the tree and jump into the mild shock of the water. Climb and jump, climb and jump.

One day, Constantine jumps into the tentacles of a jellyfish. He scrambles out with red welts all over his body and runs home, screaming. Michaelis can hear him in the distance as he walks home by himself, carrying his brother's shirt. When Constantine hurts himself, he cries out at the top of his lungs, but never when he is in a fight, or beating Michaelis, or when Dirk loses his temper.

Dirk is always home, sitting in the living room, watching television, smoking his pipe, reading the newspaper to find work. Straw tiles again cover the old carpet and fill the house with a barn smell. It's the smell of new beginnings. You smell it more at night, when you lie in bed. The tiles are meant to make every house feel like the same home, like wherever they go they are carrying the most important part with them.

The ceiling of the unit is low with a crumbed concrete texture, like a giant yellow fish finger. He sleeps on the bottom bunk; Constantine has decided that the top is better. When Michaelis goes to sleep, he hears Constantine's fingers tapping soft, sustained drum lines. A torn flap at the bottom of the flyscreen flutters with the breeze. Inside the house, down the corridor and over the stop-start wailing of Jonno, Dirk and Mum are arguing.

On Sunday nights, Con and Michaelis have a radio on and they roll in their beds to the songs they like. They both do this, rock silently back and forth, their heads burrowing into their pillows. When did it start? Perhaps Con started doing it first—Michaelis doesn't know—but they do it now and they call it *rolling*. It makes his hair messy, but he can't help doing it. They don't talk much, but Michaelis can hear his brother down below him, the creak of his bed in the darkness. It's like they're inmates in a World War II prison camp, listening to the outside world, moving nowhere in small, frustrated rhythms. They listen to the top forty.

After dinner, Constantine and Michaelis wash the dishes. Constantine decides what job he wants and Michaelis takes the other. Sometimes drying is better, sometimes washing. Constantine's eyes are fixed on something hidden, his mouth set. They stand side by side and they sweat and stare into the blackness through the window above the sink. Sometimes they drop something and it shatters and Dirk is there with his *verdomme* and his large hands to punish them for being idiots.

Michaelis has no idea what they are doing here, what they are looking for, why they left Newcastle. He asks Mum.

She doesn't look at him. 'I needed a change.'

Out the back of the house lies a sandy scrubland that is deserted during the day. But each morning when Michaelis goes there, he sees the tracks of animals— wallabies, birds, foxes, snakes—scrawling off in every direction. There is an indentation in this wasteland, the size of half a football field, like a bowl, with cracked earth at the centre. When the rain comes, after weeks and weeks of heat and sun and hardly any breeze, it belts down for days, plums of water bursting from the sky and rattling the windows.

The basin becomes a lake. Michaelis goes in as far as his waist, checks that no one is around, then takes off his swimmers so that his balls float beneath him. He swims around with his shorts in his teeth. The water tastes sweet. The hum of insects gathers around him and he lets his gaze drift into the saltbush and shrubs that form a wall between him and the nearest buildings. At the bottom of the lake, the earth has turned to clay. Michaelis dives and sinks his fists into it. He emerges from the water with the clay in his hands and tries making bowls on the shore. They fall apart.

Everything at home is falling apart, too. Although the grey carpet is covered in straw tiling, no one can cover the strange, crumbling ceiling. The shower door has three panels that are meant to slide across, but they get stuck all the time. Michaelis turns the shower off and tries to open the door. It jams, the second against the third, which comes off its hinges at the bottom.

Constantine comes into the bathroom.

'It's stuck,' Michaelis says. 'I can't move it.'

'Yeah?' Constantine examines the door, then backs away with a smile on his face.

As he leaves, he closes the door and turns off the light. Michaelis can't see his own hands and all of the horror stories he has ever heard and all the movies he's seen come rushing into his head. He thinks of the Blob, squeezing up from the blackness of the drain between his feet, dissolving skin and muscle and bone. A desperate strength possesses him. He wrenches at the panels until they clatter off their hinges and leaps over them. He flings open the door and lurches into the light. A chair creaks in the living room. Dirk comes down the corridor, shoulders him aside, stares in at the shower screen with a crack down its length, lying on the floor. He takes off one workboot.

Michaelis drops to the ground and lifts his hands.

'Don't, please don't! Constantine turned off the light!'

Dirk looks down at him with contempt. '*Stomme idioot!* When will you stop acting like a little girl?'

After he's done with Michaelis, he walks out looking for Constantine. Mum is somewhere in the background, crying and telling Dirk to stop, but Dirk never stops, not until he's finished.

~

Drifting in on the wind and tide come huge crowds of bluebottles. They cluster along the shore in heaps and slowly dry and pop underfoot. There is no way that Michaelis wants to stay out of the water in this heat, so he swims carefully, trying to spot the blue threads as they drift near. Jonno crawls across the bluebottles on the shore, popping them with his knees. He picks a fresh one up and swallows it whole and everyone has to go across the bridge, back to the mainland, to the hospital.

'It happened so quickly,' Mum says. 'One minute he is right there, and then the next...'

Dirk jerks one finger at his temple. 'You're not paying attention, *verdomme*, caught up in that head of yours.'

On the fifth of December, they celebrate St Nicholas Day. This is when you get presents back in Holland, not Christmas.

'*Sinterklaas* is the real name for Santa Claus. These people just don't know it.' Mum puts on a record of St Nicholas songs that she brought all the way from Holland and they sing together through the hiss and crackle of the strange words.

'*Hoor wie klopt daar kinderen.*'

Michaelis misses half of the words, but the rhythm carries him along.

Then Dirk has to go out for tobacco. While he is gone, Mum talks about *Sinterklaas* and his Moorish helper, Black Peter. 'Wouldn't it be nice if they came all the way here to the other side of the world to visit us after three years? Or perhaps we should go back home to visit them? Would you like that, to go back home?'

Mum looks at Michaelis and Constantine and the question hangs between them. But if *Sinterklaas* comes here, he will arrive by ship, the way that he used to in Bergen op Zoom. He used to ride onto the wharf from the barge on his white horse, Black Peter holding the reins. Michaelis can't remember when he saw it, but he can recall *Sinterklaas*'s white gloves resting against the grey mane of the horse, his silver beard down to his waist, and the velvety red folds of his cloak, edged in gold.

Black Peter carries a bag full of sweets across one shoulder. Chocolate, *taaitaai*, liquorice, things made out of different kinds of marshmallow, lots of pepper nuts—which aren't really nuts at all, but spicy biscuits the size of pebbles. You can't unravel the flavours in those biscuits. They are strange, contradictory; they shouldn't taste good. If you sing the songs for long enough, back in Bergen op Zoom, Black Peter will knock on your door and throw in the sweets.

They sing along, above the deafening rattle of insects and frogs, hoping and waiting in the humidity and heat of a summer evening, and then all at once a startling rap shakes the door, a black hand flashes into view, and in come flying handfuls of sweets, skittering across the floor, and you are scrambling as if there is no heat and no crowded darkness and no Bribie Island, just you and your brother and all of those things from home.

The only one who misses out is Dirk. Mum says this doesn't matter.

'Dirk had his chance to dive for sweets when he was a little boy.'

Dirk as a little boy. It is not as hard to imagine as you might think, not when you see him at the dinner table, measuring the servings on the plates with rapid movements of his eyes while his mouth tugs downwards at the corners. He looks much younger then, a little scared. But when his gaze swivels to yours, his fork poised to strike the hand that reaches for food too soon, the boy is gone.

~

Nikki and his parents, Susan and Paul, have come to visit from Newcastle. They all go on a daytrip out to the Big Pineapple. Pineapple plants lean in sullen, leafy ranks across the hills. Michaelis and Nikki get away from everyone and wander around the souvenir shop looking at small plastic pineapples on key rings and bottles full of sand arranged in coloured layers.

Nikki picks up and puts down a range of jars full of coloured sand. 'We might be coming up here to live.'

'My mum hates it here,' Michaelis tells him.

Mum has started saying this all the time. She'll be staring into space with a cigarette dangling from her slack mouth, and it comes out like a sigh.

Nikki buys two small vials of the coloured sand. Different colours in rippling layers, one on top of the other. He offers Michaelis one of the vials.

'Here, you want this?'

Nikki always buys things and gives them away without a second thought. All Michaelis has to do is make sure Mum doesn't find out.

Then there's a commotion outside. An ambulance has pulled up, flashing lights, crowd gathering around. The two of them walk over to have a closer look.

Susan appears before them, her face harassed. 'There you are, boys!'

Two men are wheeling a trolley towards the ambulance, a woman on it, crying and screaming, like she's about to be buried alive, arms flailing, the paramedics trying to restrain her, lots of onlookers. The woman is Mum.

Constantine comes and stands beside them, observing

it all with a bored look. 'What happened?'

'I think she's had a panic attack,' Susan says. 'It's stress. And heat. She's never handled the heat well.'

The Big Pineapple looms behind them, a fat, round, three-storey fibreglass pineapple, blazing in the sunlight against a plantation backdrop. There is big everything in Australia. You see it when you drive from one place to another, along the winding highways. The Big Prawn, the Big Banana, the Big Sheep, the Big Shearer, even the Big Mosquito, which sat on the edge of swampland near where they used to live, back in Newcastle. Giant versions of ordinary things, along roads that never seem to end. The souvenir shop is built into the pineapple's base. People shuffle and murmur through it, through the sickly sweet smell of pineapple jam and pineapple chutney and the lingering odour of their own bodies and the ones that have come before. Michaelis runs his fingers along the sand-filled vial in his pocket.

Susan puts a hand on his shoulder. 'Your mother's had a hard life. I don't know how she got through it all.'

Michaelis thinks of what Dirk says about Mum sometimes. That she's weak, unstable. Dirk will say those things as he taps his skull with one finger. People always tell Michaelis he looks like his mother. He glimpses her raving inside the ambulance before they close the doors and wonders if the panic will attack him one day, too.

'Come on, boys,' Susan tells them. 'Let's go home.'

One moment, Mum is taken off in an ambulance, the next it feels like nothing has happened. A room in their unit is stacked with packed boxes and furniture. Michaelis shows it to Nikki and they stand side by side, telling stories and comparing their penises, oblivious to the meaning of all the goods stacked in the room. But later, he wonders. Are they moving again? Is this stuff they just haven't got round to unpacking after the last time?

They go to see a bushfire, on another part of the island, with crowds of onlookers and grimy-faced firefighters directing spouts of water into the flames and the smoke. Mum watches with Jonno in her arms, in the shadow of Dirk, who stands there clamping his pipe from one end of his mouth to the other. Michaelis sits on Dirk's shoulders. He sees the sweat gathering between the curls of Dirk's hair. Livid thumbprints of ash turn end over end through the haze, past him and over him, and one spirals down to settle against Jonno's fleshy, exposed leg. Jonno does not react at first, then his body snaps into life, and he breaks into a terrible screaming.

Michaelis thinks of all this late at night, with sleep impossibly far away and all the tiny noises of the night outside against his ear, and Mum pacing and Dirk snoring, and Jonno's crying breaking out from that every now and again. Dirk can sleep through anything. When Dirk shifts in bed, it's like a train pulling out of a station.

'It's too hard,' Mum says as she rocks Jonno from side to side, cradling the phone between her shoulder and ear, the morning light already thick around her ankles. Mum is speaking in Dutch. Words dug out of the ground. 'You can't live in a country without family around you. It's too hard. You can only put up with it for so long. *Verschrikkelijk*.'

Michaelis sneaks off. He wanders along the edge of the ocean. Spotted sharks and rays swim lazily through the rocky shallows in the drawn-out light. The water near the shore is so clear it almost isn't there. Further out it gets dark and blue. One of the old fishermen told him that there are enough sharks in the nearby waters to eat everyone on the island. Michaelis imagines the rasping sound of sharks dragging themselves onto the land in search of food at night.

He always comes back for dinner. Mum insists that everyone should eat at the table, not in front of the television like some families. Dirk makes sure no one is late.

'We have some news,' Mum tells them as she places dinner on the table and starts serving it out. 'We're going back.'

'Back?' Constantine asks. 'To Newcastle?'

But that is not the answer.

5

'Snow is just around the corner. Can you feel it?'

Moessie's soft bosom heaves as she speaks. She still has her heavy furniture and her old paintings but she doesn't have her white dog anymore, only a photo. Baasje. She still keeps her snowy white hair cropped short and she lives in the same apartment that looks out over Bergen op Zoom. The Zoom is the steely river that flows through the town. It freezes in winter and people skate across the surface.

Michaelis's skin in the mirror is tanned as dark as Moessie's furniture. His feet are toughened and etched with scratches from going barefoot on Bribie Island. He can still feel the soft tar road beneath his feet, the sand and the mangrove mud squelching up between his toes. He cannot even imagine what snow feels like; he knows only that one is the past and that the other is the future.

Inside the apartment it is warm enough to wear a T-shirt. Heat radiates from the walls. Everything is built here with the cold in mind. Moessie gets out her china tea set, boils the water, and heats up the pot before she pours in the tea. You always have to heat the pot, she says in her tremulous voice. And you pour your guest the last tea and the first coffee. On the other side of the world, Mum would say it in Dutch:

Wie zijn gasten wil bedenken,
moet hemzelf het eerste thee
en het laatste koffie schenken.

It used to sound out of place in Australia. Now Michaelis feels out of place hearing it. Moessie spoons tea-leaves into a porcelain pot with an ancient silver spoon. Her hand trembles as she picks up the kettle. The skin of her wrist is like thick, soft tissue. When the water hits the tea, the smoky aroma fills the apartment. Moessie takes out a tin, opens it, and leans towards him stiffly. Inside are the chocolates Michaelis remembers, wrapped in brown and gold paper, with the gold elephant on the side.

'It's so nice to have you all back.'

'Yes, it's lovely to *be* back,' Mum says. '*Gezellig.*'

Dirk laughs. Michaelis and Con sit together on a couch. They are always closer when they come to a new place. Michaelis unwraps his chocolate and sticks it in his mouth. He lets it sit there on his tongue and melt. He gets a cup of tea as well, milky and sweet from too many cubes of sugar. He sticks a spare cube of sugar in his mouth. Dirk raps him on the knuckles with his spoon.

'It's all right,' Moessie says, folding her fleshy wrists across her belly. 'I don't mind.'

'It's the principle.' Dirk turns back to his pipe, pats down the tobacco with his thumb and sticks the pipe in his mouth, squinting down at it as he teases the tangled leaf with his lighter. Smoke drifts from his mouth. His legs stretch out before him, the workboots scarred and flecked with paint. He loosens his belt and sits there, quietly letting off smoke.

Moessie clears her throat. 'Have the boys seen their father yet?'

'Not yet.'

'He comes by here sometimes. He's very excited to see them.'

Mum's teacup rattles back onto the saucer. 'He comes *here*?'

Moessie gives a slight shrug. 'I can hardly turn him away, can I? He's always treated me very well. It's not been easy on him either, the way you went, just like that. No word to him for three years.'

'You know it wasn't like that.'

'What do I know?' Moessie lifts and drops her heavy shoulders.

Michaelis goes to the window and stares outside. Parkland stretches to the right, bare trees in rows. The salmon-pink curve of a bike path follows the lake and straightens towards the town centre. There are bike paths everywhere, following the roads like ghosts. Clusters of bikes are parked below. They all look the same, the bikes.

They don't have any gears, because everywhere it is flat. There isn't a single mountain on the horizon.

Houses huddle on the other side of the park, and past them, the distant, familiar figure of the cathedral with the giant clock. The Pepper Shaker. *De Peperbus*. But directly in front there is another apartment block, exactly the same as this one, the same balconies and dark, gleaming windows.

That's where Dad lives now.

When they flew into Amsterdam, friends of Mum met them at the airport. There was lots of crying and hugging. The man and woman then turned to stare at Michaelis, and exclaimed how tall and dark he'd become.

'You must remember Bart and Rie!' Mum said. 'They looked after you for a few months when you were young.'

He studied them with renewed interest, but nothing sparked in his memory. They have a son, a slightly built kid with a confident, easy way about him. Sebastiaan, the boy is called. He used to be his friend, apparently. The boy's mother said that they would have to be friends again. They shook hands while their mothers looked on.

They are staying with Bart, Rie and Sebastiaan while they look for a place of their own. The only good thing about this is the *Playboys* that Bart keeps by month and year on a bookshelf in the attic. Michaelis leafs through them sometimes, staring at breasts and the hair between the women's legs caught in the hazy light of the lens. The back of his neck becomes hot, like bad things could happen at any moment. Somewhere, a woman in the house is crying. He keeps flicking through the pages of the magazine, smelling the ink, the gloss, a part of him snagged on that sobbing, which is coming, he thinks, from the room Mum shares with Dirk.

It is not their home, but he has to act as though it is, just like he has to treat Dirk as his father, and he does not really like Sebastiaan, who won't share his toys and cries too easily for a boy. When Mum buys Michaelis and Con a BMX bicycle each, Rie takes her aside and complains that she has made Sebastiaan cry, that Sebastiaan feels left out and needs one too.

'The whole thing is so disappointing,' Mum says as she pulls down the sun visor in the car and checks her make-up.

She is talking about the whole experience of seeing her friends again, talking to Dirk, although Michaelis and Con and Jonno are also sitting there in the car. Inside the car, Mum speaks in a way that she can't in the house.

'Things are never the same as when you leave them. Living on top of each other, relying on the hospitality of others. They've changed. Everyone changes. I don't know if any of this was a good idea after all.'

'*Verdomme*,' Dirk says. 'Now you tell me.'

And there are so many relatives to visit, all of them waiting their turn. They have to start somewhere.

Mum glances back at Con and Michaelis, sitting either side of Jonno, who has fallen asleep. 'I was the second youngest. Jannie was the youngest. When she was born, they put me out of the pram and I had to walk. I was three. That's how I remember it. See here—' She shows them her arm, points at a white thread of raised skin above the inner wrist. 'We were sitting at the table when we were young. Jannie said she loved me and stuck a fork in my arm. It stood straight up.'

Dirk shakes his head. 'Your sister is mad. They're all mad.'

Mum drops her arm and turns to the front. 'I prefer not to hold grudges.'

Jannie's house is across the road from a park. The house is joined to a hundred other houses that stretch along the length of the street, and on the other side is the park, very green like all the parks in this town. They get out of the car, breathing mist over their scarves.

'Mind what you say,' Mum says quietly, her breath a fog.

Michaelis feels unsteady, a burning in his throat. Maybe this is how it feels when you go to a different country, when you get off a plane and everything is upside down. They go inside and meet Mum's sister and have chicken soup.

After lunch, Jannie's husband pulls out his record collection. There are lots by the Beatles; two in particular catch Michaelis's attention. One is blue, the other red. On the blue album the Beatles have long hair, and on the red one they don't. The date on the albums is 1973, two years before he was born, the time when Mum and Con and Dad were together in London, although mainly it was Mum and Con who spent the time together while Dad was out. Con used to get up in the morning and the first thing he'd do was ask for a cup of tea, which Mum made for him with lots of milk. Tea? he'd ask. Tea? They had such fun together, Mum and Con, just the two of them. Now Con doesn't like tea at all.

Michaelis sits there beside Constantine, looking at the record covers, and conversation winds and unwinds around him and he doesn't pay attention. He listens briefly when he hears Dad's name mentioned. Andreas.

'He's a wonderful man,' Jannie says. 'We've become great friends. Oh, he makes me laugh!'

'That's one side of him,' Mum says.

'Yes, yes, we all have versions of events, *stories* to tell.'

'Stories?' Mum says. 'Is that what you think they are?'

Michaelis turns back to the pictures of the Beatles. They are standing on a balcony, looking down, smiling.

'It's time to go,' Mum says. 'We won't keep you any longer.'

Jannie gives Michaelis a kiss on the way out. She's short like Mum, but she doesn't so much smile as draw back her lips from her teeth, and Michaelis keeps imagining her with a fork in her hand, ready to strike.

He and Con get in the car and Dirk slides into the front seat, filling the cabin with his breath. Con begins tapping restlessly on the hand rest of the car door. Mum is still inside. When she comes out, Jannie comes out too. Jannie has a hand in Mum's hair and pulls on it like she's trying to wrestle a handbag off a mugger.

'You're sick!' Jannie shrieks. 'You're possessed by the devil!'

Mum punches Jannie in the face to make her let go.

Dirk jumps from the front seat and bundles Mum into the car. Jannie's husband is trying to restrain her, but she struggles free and walks towards the car. She is still screaming and shaking her fist as their car turns the corner. They drive for a while without anyone speaking.

'Well, that was pleasant,' Dirk says.

'Why did she get so angry?' Michaelis's question falls into the silence of the car. He decides Mum isn't going to answer, but then she does.

'It's because we have different memories.'

~

He is seven. Eight is not so far away. By the time they get home that evening, he knows that he is sick. His face is burning. His cheeks have grown tight and swollen. Mum puts a cool hand on his face.

'I think you need to go upstairs and lie in bed.'

It doesn't help. His cheeks feel as if they are about to

explode. Every time he swallows he feels needles in his eardrums. He hears them speaking downstairs.

'*Hij heeft de bof.*'

De bof. The mumps. He can smell straw. The world is moving and moving. The house hardly exists. He moans, and when he closes his eyes he sees a black dog lying on a hot road, bleeding from its mouth, whining, tongue half out, dark flecks on its exposed gums. *Barry will be okay, soon as I go.* He's remembering that wrong; Barry got away. Didn't he?

Dirk is standing over him. 'What's wrong with you? Stop making all of that noise. *Aansteller. Kleine meisje.* Stop making more of it than what it is.'

Dirk lifts one hand, then drops it again. His feet thud down the stairs, down into the jumbled haze of noise beneath. Michaelis draws the blanket over his head. He drifts through pain and finds himself back on Bribie Island. They have not left at all. He is daydreaming, walking along the road. Low rumbles carry from the horizon. Toads flattened by cars bake in the sun, clouds of blood around each one. Razors in his mouth, pressed up against his cheeks, digging out towards his ears. Stories. Dad is still far away. The road leads to the beach, a dense wall of mangroves to one side, with countless roots. The shore slopes away so gradually that the water hardly seems to be getting deeper, but it is, and there are sharks in there, dark shapes beneath the surface, waiting to come onto the land.

6

The same thick hair rises from his head, combed back in a wave, but silvery streaks run through it. His skin has an ashen look—not enough sun, he says with an easy laugh—and everything is angular in his face. Dad hugs them both and gives them a kiss. Michaelis smells cologne, feels that rough scrape of freshly shaven cheek.

'It's so good to see you both! Gosh, you are both so *dark*, like proper little Greeks! Animaaales!' Dad keeps speaking in his high-pitched, rapid voice. 'Not bad, eh? I've got my own car. Your dad's doing pretty well for himself, isn't he? I can't believe that you're back. You have to tell me everything.'

'Make sure you look after them.'

Dad doesn't look at Mum. 'Of course, of course.'

He speaks in English, like they do, but with an accent all his own, a slippery sort of thing, caught between a handful of languages and places. They get in the car, Constantine in the front, Michaelis in the back.

'You still playing football, Constantinos?'

'Yeah.'

Dad laughs and shakes his head. 'Good, good. We'll have to see if you can still steal the ball off me. I have to warn you, I've been practising. I won't be easy on you. You look almost like a man now, Constantinos. Incredible. Incredaaaable! How does it feel, to be nearly a man?'

Con is silent. Dad has perfectly shaped teeth, like Constantine's, but they are yellowish from all the smoking that he does. A cigarette hangs from his mouth, and though he blows the smoke through the window, it gets sucked back in. The car is old and uncomfortable, like every other car Michaelis has been in, and he still feels weak from the mumps. He stares at the back of the front seat, feeling the car lurch around unexpected corners.

'Been seeing any girls, Constantinos?'

Constantine doesn't answer.

Dad pokes him in the ribs. 'Well then, Constantinos? Any nice Greek girls, eh? Handsome young man like you...'

'No.'

Dad puts a hand on his shoulder, squeezes it. 'Oh, sure you have. Are you keeping things from your father? Your own flesh and blood?'

Con turns to look at him, his face hard. 'I told you *no*.'

'Okay then. Okay.' Dad takes away his hand.

He drives with the other elbow resting on the rim of the window, the creases in his leather jacket glistening at the joint, an amused glint in his eye, his fingers drumming lightly on the steering wheel.

'When the time comes,' he says in a serious tone, 'make sure you settle down with a nice Greek girl, Constantinos. They're the best.'

'I feel sick,' Michaelis says.

Dad's eyes flash into the rear-vision mirror, like he forgot Michaelis was in the back. 'What kind of sick?'

'Carsick.'

'How bad?'

'I need to vomit.'

'You get that sick from being in a car? Wait till I pull over, all right? Can you do that?'

As soon as the car door swings open, Michaelis sends the morning's food into the grass. Farmland stretches out before him. A bunch of cows stare at him with their big, sad eyes, slowly chewing their cuds. Dad is standing over him. He pinches his nose and glances around.

'Are you okay, Michaelis?'

'I'm okay.'

'You don't look okay.' Dad makes it sound like an accusation.

When they get to Dad's apartment, he gives them an ice-cream container full of almonds. 'From your grandmother in Cyprus. So, how was Australia? Did you see anything dangerous? Sharks? Snakes? Kangaroos?'

Dad's eyes constantly come to rest on Constantine.

Michaelis wants to talk about Australia and all the moving and Dirk, but somehow he doesn't say a thing. Constantine isn't saying much, either. Dad fills the silence. There is an incredible restlessness in his wiry frame.

'I want you to remember this, boys: my house is yours. You may have been on the other side of the world, but you'll always be mine.'

The whole place is tidy, though it smells of aftershave and cigarettes and coffee. Michaelis pours himself a glass of orange juice from the fridge. From the kitchen window, he can see the other apartment block, the one where Moessie lives, where he was born seven years ago. He can see her windows, although they look impenetrable from this distance.

Michaelis follows Con back into the living room. Dad comes in and surveys them both, sitting around his glass-topped coffee table, with their glasses of juice and coiled, rubbery Greek sweets and plate of chocolates.

Someone knocks at the door. Dad answers it. A boy stands there, looking up at Dad, glancing in at the apartment, shy and lean, a few years older than Constantine.

'Not now,' Dad tells the boy, ruffling his hair. 'I'll talk to you later.'

He closes the door and walks back inside.

'My sons,' he says, grinning hugely. 'My beautiful boys.'

But he has two more young children now, and a second wife, Irene, whom he has also divorced. Irene is religious, and when Dad takes them to visit their half-brother and half-sister on the edge of town, she talks about how Jesus has changed her life. She stares at them when she says this, and Michaelis is tempted to say something, to ask questions, just to keep the conversation going.

She smokes one cigarette after another, just like Dad, and as she talks about Jesus, she interrupts herself to take long drags. She makes a lunch of different cheeses and thinly sliced bacon followed by chocolate flakes on thick white bread. Her children look on. Michaelis doesn't know what to make of them. They have the same dark skin as him, and that is all.

Irene does not speak about Mum at all, but there is something in her voice when she draws near to it, a tightness that you cannot trust.

'Play with your brother and sister,' Dad tells them before he follows Irene into the kitchen.

Michaelis hears the metallic rasp of a lighter, and smoke drifts into the living room.

'Why,' he hears Irene say in a low voice, 'was this necessary?'

On the drive back, Dad is subdued. He puts a new cigarette in his mouth, lights it, and lets the smoke pour out of his wide nostrils. 'Maybe we won't do that again too soon. But it was good to see them at least once, yes?'

Michaelis and Constantine stare back at him in the rear-view mirror. Dad, who was here all the while that they were in Australia, fixed in memory, has continued living and has created a new family, as if one can simply be left behind.

~

Dirk and Mum have bought an old house which has four storeys, and which no one else wanted because it is falling apart. The fourth storey is a cavernous attic with two rooms at the front. Dirk tears out the front of the attic and puts in massive windows using a system of pulleys and a crane. Before the windows go in, he hoists in a competition-sized ping-pong table.

One of the rooms in the attic belongs to Michaelis. It's the first room that he's ever had to himself. Walking alone up four flights of stairs terrifies him. Dirk will make him walk up by himself at night, and he isn't allowed to turn on the light. He isn't so scared of sleeping alone in that room, though—a streetlight shines into the window. And the street beyond the window is busy. On wet evenings you can stare outside at light glimmering and vanishing and reappearing on the slick road between the cars.

When Dirk is not working on the house, he is at work, and comes home covered in paint and dust. He is a foreman again, building things that Michaelis never sees.

Dirk goes to work while Mum looks after Jonno and does things around the house or sits there with her cup of coffee, listening to records—Neil Young, Neil Sedaka, the Beach Boys, the Mamas and the Papas; records that she carried from Holland to Australia and back again. The crackle of their voices fills the house as she stares out into the garden without seeing it.

One day Mum answers the front door and there is an old woman there. She looks apologetic.

'I don't mean to interfere,' the woman says, 'but there's a baby on your roof.'

And there Jonno is, in the broad guttering, laughing and peering down at the street, four storeys below. He must have climbed from Michaelis's chair to his desk and out the window. While Michaelis watches, Mum leans on the desk and coaxes Jonno inside with a piece of Lego.

'I feel so terrible,' Mum says. 'I get so easily distracted.'

She goes into the living room and stares off into space, Jonno in her arms, patting his back.

There isn't room for a dog, but they own a rabbit for a short time, a small grey thing with floppy ears. They keep it in a cage at the back of the house, and let it out in the afternoons, so that it can hop silently around the living room. Michaelis comes home from school one day and the cage is empty.

'The rabbit is gone,' Mum tells him simply.

'Where?'

'Off to a better place.'

Michaelis doesn't believe her. 'Where, Mum?'

'In the backyard,' Dirk says flatly, staring down at him over his beard. 'Jonno tried to give it a shower and broke its neck.'

Michaelis stares at Dirk for a moment longer, a knot of anger in his stomach. If he'd done that, he'd be lying in bed right now trying to ignore the fire in his arse. Jonno is in a world of his own, one with different rules. Dirk doesn't touch him. It's because Jonno is Dirk's real son.

Michaelis watches his younger brother sometimes, the same large forehead as Dirk, the same heavy gaze when he focuses on some game.

'He's only two,' Mum says. 'He doesn't know these things. He was just trying to help. I was on the phone and I didn't realise what was happening. I'm sorry. Don't be angry. We'll get something else.'

Maybe it is Michaelis. Maybe it is the anger he feels, the sense of rage that rises in him sometimes when he looks at Dirk, but he can't forgive Jonno as easily as everyone else does.

Michaelis has joined the Cub Scouts, and made a friend who is a year older. Max has blond hair that hangs to his shoulders, almost translucent skin and an air of separation from the crowd.

They go on a camping trip with the troop. Michaelis is used to trips into the bush taking hours and ending in wilderness, but they hardly drive at all and end up staying at a farm for a night. When all the kids are called out for activities, Max and Michaelis hide inside.

'We should do something *really* fun,' Max says.

They climb into the roof of the farm building and jump from beam to beam, tempting their luck, until Michaelis misses a beam and breaks through the roof. Chunks of plaster rain down into a kitchen below, and startled faces look up at him, dangling there by his hands, until he pulls himself back up into the roof.

Max swears at him. 'We're done for now,' he says. 'We're done for.'

They are taken to see the Scoutmaster.

'We don't need people with your attitude here,' he tells them. 'Your fathers are coming to pick you up.'

Michaelis becomes aware of every part of his body when he hears this. Something is twisting in his stomach, making everything feel weak. His spine is tingling; his buttocks have tightened. All there is to do now is wait for Dirk to turn up. Like when you say the word *lemon* and your mouth waters.

When the top level of the house is finished, they go to a special restaurant to celebrate. The Cauliflower. They know the restaurant is special because you have to wait so long for food to come out.

'Get your elbows off the table!'

Constantine has moved before the words are out of Dirk's mouth. He never needs to be told anything twice. Michaelis stares past him to the window with the slender trees marching off beyond the panes into the darkness.

'Michaelis. *Michaelis!*' Dirk is wearing his workboots. Michaelis knows it the moment he gets a kick in his shin. His knees jerk and his legs thump at the table. Heat gathers in his ears and around his neck.

A couple at the next table look across. Dirk doesn't take his eyes from Michaelis. 'Are you a little girl? No? Then why are you crossing your legs under the table?'

'Oh, Dirk, what does it matter?' Mum says.

'Because I tell him, that's why.'

'How do you even *know* what he does with his legs under the table? This is supposed to be a celebration.'

'You let him get away with too much. It won't do him any favours.'

Michaelis separates his legs. He leans on the table, catches Dirk's eye and pulls his elbows back before Dirk can react, Con grinning in the background.

That night, before he goes to sleep, Mum sits beside him on the bed and strokes his hair for a while. 'Your grandfather used to cross his legs. He loved to read too, just like you, and he was very clever. You would have liked him.'

Michaelis doesn't say anything. He loves it when Mum strokes his hair, and yet he feels sad too, because he knows that it never lasts. And before too long, he is alone again in the darkness.

~

'Blood,' Constantine says, pointing at the tank. 'A round went right in there and blew them up.'

The war museum is not what Michaelis expected. The path has led them through the forest from one broken war machine to another. They are drawing near the end. The stain around the hole in the tank looks like rust. A spring coils through the darkness inside.

'Come on then,' Mum says.

Michaelis hesitates. 'Did people really die here?'

'Maybe.'

Dirk laughs. 'They dragged this here after the war. For some stupid reason, people want to look at it.'

Mum folds her arms across her chest. 'Other people are always stupid, according to you.'

'I know what I know. It's obvious.'

'Well, I want to see them.'

Sometimes these exchanges lead to an argument, but not today. They walk to a building at the end of the path and step through the door into a strange heaviness. A wall curves the whole way round the inside. Black and white photographs hang along the wall. Jews. *Joden*. He has heard that name often. Mum talks about them. She's always watching documentaries about World War II.

Michaelis doesn't know much about what happened to the Jews, only that they were taken away in trucks, that they disappeared during the war from the neighbourhood in which Mum later grew up. There is a familiarity to the word, though, and he has wondered in the past whether they are Jews themselves. No, Mum assures him, they are Roman Catholics.

In some photos, the *Joden* are naked and dead and piled on top of one another, like misshapen candles. In other pictures, they are alive, but they don't look much better. Everything on them has shrunk, except their teeth and their eyes. The people Michaelis pities most are standing in queues. They are waiting to be killed. Seeing doomed people is worse than seeing dead people. Michaelis wants to reach into the huge pictures and yank those people out of their fate. There are ovens and chimneys spewing out thick, black smoke.

'The Nazis made them into soap.' Constantine stands at his shoulder. He sounds like he's telling stories of vampires and werewolves. 'When the Germans weren't making them into soap, they burned them in the ovens.'

'It wasn't just the Germans,' Mum says. 'Lots of people got involved. Lots of people from other countries were also Nazis, or agreed with them. They couldn't have done all of that alone.'

Michaelis tugs at Mum's hand. 'How can people do that?'

'They can do lots of things.'

As he settles into bed that night, Michaelis wonders how soap can be made out of people. He wonders what *his* soap is made out of.

'Why didn't people help them?'

Mum pauses at the light switch. 'Some tried. A lot just pretended it wasn't happening. They got on with things or even took advantage of it.'

'Why did we go there today?'

'It's important to know what happened.'

'Why?'

'I don't know…If enough people know, if they really know about that sort of thing, maybe it won't happen again.'

'Leave the door open?' he says.

'A little,' she answers. 'Just a little.'

When Mum is gone, Michaelis lies in the darkness thinking about what she said. He doesn't understand. He doesn't understand how knowing about something can stop it from happening again. It's never been that way for him. Like when he crosses his legs under the table. He's eight and he's been doing it forever. When he crosses his legs, Dirk kicks him in the shin. Once the pain has died down, Michaelis just does the same thing again.

It is called forgetting.

The house is constantly changing, level by level, and when you don't pay attention, it changes more rapidly.

When Dirk isn't at work, he's tearing up floors and stripping walls and building stuff, painting cornices, smoothing over holes, pressing in tiles. The boys have to help, carrying buckets and wheelbarrows of rubbish outside, collecting nails, scraping away wallpaper from the old walls. At other times, Dirk makes things for Con and Michaelis: wooden swords, and boxes to put stuff in. He hands them over without a word.

The house becomes magnificent, with wooden tiles laid perfectly along the bottom level, the windows opening smoothly and lightly, lacquered wood everywhere—bookshelves, tables, cupboards—all springing from his hands and filling the house with marvellous life. There is no problem that he can't solve with his hands.

And Constantine has become the best football player on his team. In Australia he was brilliant at cricket; here he is brilliant at football and surrounded by a new group of friends who admire him. His room is plastered with soccer posters. His hero, Johan Cruyff, is there on the wall, playing for Ajax, playing for Feyenoord, playing for Holland. Con can turn on the ball exactly like Cruyff does. He practises it on the street outside their house, then kicks flat and hard at the wall. Michaelis has never seen Con in a game. Mum doesn't go to things like that. Con rides there on his bike. Dad goes to the games, though, every week. Michaelis knows this because Con talks about it to Mum.

'I don't want him there,' Con says.

'Why?'

'I just want to play and not have to think about him.'

Something strained creeps into Mum's voice. 'Has he done anything? Did he say something to you?'

'No.' Con falls silent for a moment. 'He talks to my friends.'

'And?'

'I don't know. He acts like they're *his* friends.'

'I'll tell him to stop going, then.'

Michaelis gets a kitten for his ninth birthday. He calls it Ed. He's black with a streak of white on his neck, like a bow tie, and he sleeps in Michaelis's bed at night: a small, soft engine of noise and warmth.

Con often goes off alone, fishing, just like he used to do on Bribie Island, although now he goes into damp, cool wetlands where he's after carp, huge fish that take a long time to surrender. He takes a fibreglass rod, leans it back over his shoulder and rides off for the day. He never comes back with fish. You have to rip the hook out from the thick, fleshy lips of the carp and throw them back into the muddy water. The fish don't feel anything. They keep swimming through the darkness until they're caught again. He goes only for the fight.

Winter returns. Mornings, Michaelis jumps on his bike—a different, larger one, second-hand, because the last one was stolen. All the bikes in the neighbourhood look the same and they are always getting stolen—by kids, by drunk people coming home at night, by the gypsies who live in the trailer park just out of town. When it is still dark and foggy, you pedal along the icy street towards school, lungs aching, the pant of breath in your ear, the whir of the light generator on the tyre. Sometimes you slide on the ice and fall and your hands hurt in the cold.

At school, things aren't so bad. They don't wear uniforms here. Michaelis calls teachers by their first names. They get disappointed rather than angry, even the time he disappeared into the nearby wetlands at lunchtime and came back covered from head to toe in mud. That was the summer just passed, and right now St Nicholas Day is drawing near again, so it begins to get gloomy towards the end of the school day and they all sing St Nicholas songs in the classroom until Black Peter knocks on the door and throws sweets into the room, everyone giggling and panting and grasping on the floor. Dutch sweets. One of the girls wrote him a Christmas card and he has shoved it in his pocket. He scrambles on his knees on the floor, and worries for a moment that if he looks up, he will see the cramped insides of the unit on Bribie Island.

Con and Michaelis go out some afternoons and play in a nearby park, which is vast and arranged around a small lake. In summer the grass is dark green, but now everything is buried in white and the trees are shadows, and when he talks, his voice feels like the only living thing in the world.

'I wish I could run like you,' Michaelis says as they drag their sled up a hill.

Con is in a good mood. He smiles across at Michaelis. 'You will, one day.'

They're riding the sled down the hill and braking at the bottom, near the ice-covered lake. The trick is to pull only on one brake so that the sled digs into the snow as it turns.

Michaelis is half in the sled. 'I wish Dad liked me as much as you.'

Something twists in Con's expression. 'That's because you're an idiot.'

Before Michaelis can answer, Con shoves him, and Michaelis shoots down the hill. At the bottom he doesn't brake properly and goes skating over the ice on the lake. With a crisp, rippling splinter he crashes through. The water slaps the heat out of his lungs. He starts swimming for the shore.

Constantine is there, waiting. 'Get the sled. Go back and get the fucking sled.'

Michaelis swims back through the ice, breaking it with his strokes until he reaches the sled. When he finally makes it out of the water, he is shaking so violently that he can't hold the sled. They walk home, Michaelis shivering and wary. They turn into their street. The front door is there ahead of them.

'You never pay attention,' Con says.

Michaelis doesn't know what to say. Michaelis loves Constantine as much as he loves his father, in the same aggrieved, unsatisfied way. The few times that they see Dad out in the park for a few hours, to kick a soccer ball, or when they go for something to eat, things always follow the same pattern. No mention is made of their brother and sister, or of Mum, and for a brief moment it seems like they are just like other boys out for the day with their father. Except that Constantine is surly and withdrawn and Michaelis is shrill and eager. He knows that he is awkward in his eagerness, but he can't stop. Dad hardly notices him, anyway.

'They would love you in Greece,' Dad says sometimes, fixing Constantine with a brilliant stare, as if it is just the two of them alone together. 'You're a beautiful boy, Constantinos. Maybe one day I'll show you Greece.'

~

From the beginning, Michaelis has called him only by his first name. He is married to Mum, but Dirk will never be his father.

'Go get some milk.' Dirk thrusts money into Michaelis's outstretched hand.

Michaelis walks to the store. Night comes quickly in the winter, like a door closing. The street lamps pump misty light into the evening. On his way back past the park with the milk in his hand, he stops and stares across the lake. The ice is a hard, slippery shell that sits over the blackness and thickens with each night. There are leaves out there, brown or flame-coloured, caught in the surface, and there are orange fish—gold carp—lying on their sides, staring up at the grey sky with cloudy, alarmed eyes. You wouldn't fall through anymore.

He suddenly has a bright, jagged memory of digging a hole at the beach, with the swirling sound of the surf and children screaming and the air smelling of suncream and vinegar and salt. He unscrews the milk, takes a mouthful. The milk tastes good out here, in the cold. He's like an explorer, drinking his ration. He screws the lid back on very tightly, lets the light of the street lamps fall into the bottle, across the surface of the milk. It doesn't look like he's taken any, but a familiar weight seeps into him as he walks home.

He knocks on the front door.

Dirk opens it, stares down at him over his beard. 'Did you drink any?'

Michaelis watches his brother lie all the time. The way to lie is to empty your face, to believe yourself, and to not look for reassurance.

He meets Dirk's eyes. 'No.'

Dirk swipes him with one hand and then lifts him by the hair. 'Idiot. Liar. Look at yourself in the mirror.'

And the proof is there, staring back at him, alongside the glowing red handprint on his cheek: a milk moustache.

Inside, Constantine is helping Mum bathe Jonno. Michaelis can hear their voices echoing in the bathroom, drifting up the stairs.

'I can't believe it,' Con says. 'I was this old. I can't believe that Dad would do that to someone so small, so fragile.'

'You hated me for taking you away,' Mum says. 'Do you remember? And you used to talk about wanting to come back. You talked about it all the time. I thought this was what you wanted.'

'We should have stayed in Australia. I hate it here.'

Now red welts cover his arse and his back. Not from Dirk, but from a disease. They itch like mad. He wants to scratch them, but he's not supposed to. They're *contagious*. No school, no going outside to play, no walking around. He has to lie on his belly and wait. Ed stalks in sometimes, plays at his toes and then curls up beside him.

Three times a day, Mum comes up and rubs cream into his skin. The bedsheets stick to him when he moves.

Mum is cooking downstairs, singing along with one of her records. The sound of her bustling clatters up the stairs. The album fills the walls with the cloying tones of a French singer. Edith Piaf. Mum explains the songs sometimes. One song is about death and ghosts. In the song, Edith says that she's not afraid to die. You only say things like that when you *are* afraid, Michaelis thinks. If you don't care, you just don't talk about it, like Constantine, who is afraid of nothing. He only *acts*. Anything Michaelis mentions becomes real, so he keeps silent. It's the same if he pulls the blanket to his neck at night, closes his eyes against the darkness, counts his breath. Wait. There's nothing there. *We all have stories.*

Moessie claims she once saw a UFO. It was a silver dish, with a circle of lights, and flew overhead when she was shopping in the marketplace. She was so surprised that she fell and broke her hip—but no one else saw it, except for Beatrix, who is a terrible liar, so how can you believe what *she* says? Beatrix is one of Michaelis's aunts. She has seventeen children, but Michaelis has seen none of them, because Beatrix hates Mum like a lot of her sisters do, and they have not come to see her since she returned from Australia.

'I never liked her either,' Mum admits as she rubs cream into his bottom. 'A horrible, nasty person, right from the beginning. Worse than Jannie. When I was little, after my illness, I used to have to walk to school with her. It took us an hour or so. She'd make me walk behind her, and we would hardly speak at all. I wore her old clothes, and they never fitted me well. As we got closer to school, I would slow down because there'd be a group of older kids waiting, girls in her year. They called her names, said that she was a liar and a thief and so on.

She was all of those things, but the way those other girls treated us was partly because of our family.'

'What was wrong with our family?'

'There were stories, things that happened before I was born, during the war. The kids in the neighbourhood weren't supposed to play with us. We were never invited to birthday parties. It used to outrage my mother. I remember playing by myself outside the houses where there were birthday parties, hoping they'd invite me in. I was never entirely sure if it was because I was fat or because of the stories.'

'What stories?'

'Wait.'

Mum gets up to answer the phone, and she does not come back upstairs, and Michaelis thinks how it is always like this, how so many of the stories she tells have no real endings, or they end at a different place every time. Perhaps this is why he can listen to them again and again. It doesn't matter what the endings were, because it is the past, and the last daylight is sinking from the windowpanes. A smell of meat, spicy and warm, comes from downstairs. Mum is making tomato soup with meatballs. There will be a stack of pancakes, thin as tissue paper, afterwards.

The words that Mum leaves him with fascinate Michaelis, all the dark places they touch, the way that they connect and separate like paths in a maze. He decides that when he grows up, he'll be an explorer, and he'll write about it. He'll discover every last part of the world. But he is an explorer already, whether he likes it or not. There is one difference only: he doesn't forge bravely ahead, the landscape just changes around him.

Like when he watches television and grows sleepy. His eyelids fill with lead.

'Go to bed,' Mum tells him, 'go to bed.'

But he doesn't listen. He always wants to know the next part of the story. He blinks, and when he opens his eyes, the room is black, everyone is gone—the television is a dead, empty box in front of him, the floor cold and hard beneath his back.

This is how quickly things change.

~

'We're going back,' Mum says one day.

'Where?'

'Where do you think? To Australia. That's really our home. We just needed to come back and live here for a while to realise that.' It is as if Mum is finishing a conversation that she started in her head.

Then snow turns to mud and spring comes. The bare trees fill up with leaves and Michaelis almost forgets that he'll be leaving. Days grow longer and longer until he falls asleep with the light of the day still out there. They go to farms outside town and buy crates full of fragrant strawberries and fresh milk that you have to boil to get the cream off. Sometimes Constantine takes

Michaelis exploring. Sometimes they go into places that are forbidden. Sometimes they ride their bicycles out to the strawberry fields and crawl in on their bellies and eat everything they can touch, the green light on their faces. They lie with their cheeks close to the ground, listening for the barking of the dog to change tone. The sound of gnats and flies gathers around their ears and the sun rests against their backs and strawberry juice trickles from the corners of their mouths. Michaelis eats, lost in that moment, until it's time to run.

'I've got them.' Dirk brandishes the envelope with the tickets, the aeroplane tickets, the proof that they are going back to Australia. Dirk and Mum stand there staring at one another and smiling. Whenever they know they are going somewhere, Mum and Dirk get happy for a while, like they are looking in the same direction, and there is nothing behind them. Dirk takes the tickets out of the envelope and shows them to Mum.

'Can I see?' Michaelis asks.

Dirk looks at Michaelis. The corners of his mouth drop. 'No. You'll only ruin them.'

Mum folds her hands across her chest. 'You don't have to be that way.'

'*Verdomme.* You know what he's like.'

'Why do you have to turn everything into a fight about him? Can't we just enjoy something for a change?'

'You're always on his side.'

As he walks past Con in the hallway, his brother grins and whispers, 'Well done, Michaelis, well done.'

Michaelis takes his cat upstairs, sits at the desk that Dirk built beneath his window and stares out over the street. The street is busy with afternoon traffic. The cat purrs. Michaelis thinks of how Constantine hardly gets in trouble, how he is an expert at avoiding it. Usually it only happens when he does things to Michaelis, when Michaelis calls for help, and then they both get it.

Every now and again, though, Constantine does make Dirk upset. He once told Dirk to get fucked. Dirk chased him up the road with a piece of wood. Con is fast and he got away. Later, he gets the beating, but there is always that moment where Con is running ahead of Dirk, when Dirk throws down his arms and stands gasping on the street, defeated.

~

Farmland rolls past the window, the flat, green landscape broken by skinny trees and hedges and occasional houses. The carriage rattles as it enters a bend. Claws rake through the gap in the cardboard box on his lap and his cat gives another frantic hiss in the darkness. Michaelis is taking Ed to a farm in the north of Holland, to say goodbye, to leave him forever, but first he is treating him to being trapped in a box for three hours.

'He'll love it there,' Mum says again. 'There are lots

of animals. He'll feel right at home. You'll see.'

When they get there and open the box, the cat bursts out like it's on fire and hurtles up into a pine tree. Michaelis stands under the tree for a long time, calling softly, but it does no good.

'Never mind,' Mum says, frowning up into the branches. 'We'll get you another cat in Australia.'

Michaelis's aunt is called Margreet. She is a farmer's wife. She gets up with her husband at four in the morning to milk cows. Early in the morning, the moon stares in through the glass, pale with hypothermia. Maybe this is why Margreet is such a hard-looking woman, with a downward turn in her mouth and a glint in her eye.

'That,' Mum says, 'comes from your grandmother. She's a real survivor.'

'What did she survive?'

Mum doesn't answer. She's talking to Margreet. His aunt's skull is outlined through her short, peppery hair. She gives Michaelis a present, a Lego knight on a horse. Michaelis plays with it on the polished floor. He lies on his belly with his feet under Mum's chair. He doesn't listen to most of what they are saying, but towards the end of the afternoon, a word catches his attention. *Trut.*

'She was a bitch,' Margreet says. *Een trut.*

Mum clears her throat. 'Yes, but she's still our mother.'

The Lego knight pauses in his hand, under the shadow of the chair.

Margreet snorts. 'No helping that. What makes me so angry is how she can moralise. After what she did in the war!'

The two of them fall silent. He can hear geese and chickens outside, caught up in their own babble, and a dog barking, as if there is a stranger out there, entering the property.

'We don't know,' Mum says. 'We don't know what happened.'

'Isn't that what they said about you and Andreas?'

Mum takes a deep breath before she answers. 'That was different.'

Margreet's voice goes brittle and hard when she laughs. 'How do you imagine they became so wealthy during the war? Do you think our parents were thrown into *jail* for nothing?'

'Well, no. Of course not.'

The two of them drink their tea. No light-hearted chatter here, no *gezellig*. Just breathing and the clinking of cups.

'Look,' Mum says, 'she never talked about it with me. There are things that I remember growing up with. Just a few odd events.'

'Why do you think our grandmother rejected us?'

Mum glances towards Michaelis. He makes a show of running his knight across the floor again.

'I don't know,' Mum says. 'I mean, I *do*, but I don't want to talk about it now. I didn't come here to talk about this with you.'

'That's what we do in our family. We don't talk about things—we bury them. Just like they did with *you*.'

Mum doesn't answer. There's an open fire in the corner, crackling and hissing. Michaelis stares into the fire and the glowing embers. His face near the flames is warm and his feet are cold.

Margreet's voice lowers, as if that is all it takes to make Michaelis stop listening.

'You and I both know that she still believes that rubbish about the Jews. That she still thinks Hitler was a great man. But do you know why Mother sent me away when I was born? Why she hardly had a thing to do with me for most of my life? She got raped in prison by some Canadian prison guard. I think that was my father.'

Raped. Michaelis turns the word over in his head.

Mum glances across at him again, a look of warning in her eyes. 'I didn't know that. God. I just thought that you lived somewhere else because she had so many of us to look after. I thought it was normal.'

Margreet makes a scoffing sound. 'There are a lot of things that we grew up thinking were normal.'

'Maybe she's changed since then.'

'Then why are you leaving again?'

'We shouldn't be talking about it now.'

They face one another for a moment in silence, Mum and his aunt. Beside Margreet, Mum looks particularly young, with her fuller lips, the blush on her cheeks, and the hair that comes down to her shoulders. All of his aunts have short hair, just like Moessie.

'It needs to be said,' Margreet declares. 'I'll never forgive her. You shouldn't either, after what she tried to do to you. People like that don't deserve forgiveness. She's filled our family with poison, and it's still here, in all of us.'

On the train back, he tries not to think about Moessie. He imagines that he is a king with one loyal subject, a Lego knight with an unbreakable smile. One day, he tells the knight silently, I'm going to buy a castle, and I'm going to put *you* in charge.

But they are going home. Back to Dirk, to whom all of Mum's relatives are so polite, although they don't admire him or laugh at his jokes the way that they do with Dad. Michaelis leans back in the seat and lets his imagination drift. Nothing lasts forever, not even this sensation in the pit of his stomach, the feeling of going home, the feeling of knowing things that he doesn't want to. Some things you can't change, but some things you can. He will run away, maybe when he is sixteen, and come back later. The older he gets, the more he can imagine killing Dirk.

Mum looks across at him suddenly. 'I wish your aunt hadn't said those things. She shouldn't have spoilt your grandmother for you. You only really have *one*, after all.'

Michaelis thinks of the museum with all the doomed people, and then he thinks of Moessie with her smile, and the way it makes her eyes grow small.

'But it's true, right?'

'Yes, it's true.' Mum gives a slight shake of her head. 'Of course I know she did some terrible things during the war. That's why I didn't have any friends growing up: I was the daughter of a collaborator. But my mother never regretted the choices she made during the war, only that she lost everything afterwards. In many ways she's a strong woman, your grandmother. Formidable. She has no time for weakness. She once told me that I killed my father because I dated a Jewish man. She tried to have me committed to a mental asylum after I left your father and said what he'd done, and she always stood up for him. I'll never forget how she collected me from the hospital after I overdosed on the pills. She didn't hug me or help me. She just walked ahead of me. She said that she'd let me die if I did it again.' Mum's shoulders drop. 'I love her because she's my mother, but she's not what you'd call a nice person.'

'Why did we come back here, then?'

Mum looks away, out of the window, to the passing trees and the flat, damp countryside. 'I was homesick. I try not to hold grudges. In the end, I thought you boys should know your father. My family felt the same. Your father did some terrible things, but he has his good side. I wouldn't have fallen in love with him otherwise.'

Michaelis sees his aunt Jannie again, standing in the middle of the road, shaking her fist. *You're sick. Possessed by the devil.* It is quiet in the train. A woman across the aisle looks up from her paper and then looks down again.

Mum shifts beside him and touches his arm. 'You were born out of love, you and your brother. You must never forget that.'

They are leaving and there is nothing that can be done to stop it. Michaelis and Con have already handed over their pocket money to help pay for the trip.

'You'll get it back eventually,' Mum says, 'but we need it right now.'

They have sold their house to a group of monks. Michaelis imagines the monks making themselves at home in his bedroom with all of its wooden furniture, playing each other on the ping-pong table in the attic.

But now they are to stay at Aunt Carolien's house in the north, and then they are flying out again to Australia. Carolien is the only sister Mum gets along with. When they visit each other, Carolien and Mum are always drinking wine together and laughing. Michaelis hardly ever sees Mum happy like that.

Michaelis spends a lot of time by himself in the back garden, which has a massive plum tree. One night, Dirk goes out to tell Michaelis that it is dinnertime. Michaelis forgets he's been told. He's looking for fish in the pond under the tree. Dirk comes out again. He drags Michaelis away from the pond by the hair and pins him against the wall, one hand around his throat.

'I don't want you fucking things up in Australia.' Dirk speaks softly as he makes a fist with his other hand and rests it against Michaelis's jaw. 'I don't want you being stupid and I want you to *listen*. And if you run to your mother and tell her about this, we won't talk anymore. I'll just kill you.'

Michaelis can feel the blood trapped in his head, the bruise under his jaw, the twitching jolt beneath his skin. He goes inside and sits at the table, next to Constantine. Everyone is laughing and talking. Mum is feeding Jonno, her pale face creased into a smile. Dirk sits at one end of the table, gnawing on a sausage, fat dripping into his beard. He coughs softly and says something and Carolien laughs the way that she laughs for everyone. No one can see what Michaelis sees. Or perhaps they see it and pretend not to, and forget the moment when it stares back at them.

7

The plane banks and beyond the wing the sea comes into view, flecked with white, shadows of storm clouds racing along its surface. The plane drops and Michaelis feels the lurch in his stomach. Mum reaches across and holds his hand. Dirk glances at the movement and looks away.

'There it is, Mike,' Mum says. 'There it is.'

Through the thick glass the city spreads below them. Skyscrapers in the distance, suburbs fleshed out with green, rising and falling over folds of land like clothes tossed on the ground.

'Now we keep close together,' Dirk tells them. 'I just want to get out of the airport without any stupidness, okay?'

'I'm sure we all want to get out of the airport,' Mum says.

The plane lands with a jolt. The airport slides into view. One moment it is impossible to think that you will ever stop, and the next you get sucked back as the movement bleeds away.

'I can't wait to put my feet in the ocean,' Mum says as they get out into the brisk air.

'Ah, *verdomme*, it'll be cold.'

Mum barely glances at him. 'I don't care. It will be wonderful.'

When he thinks of Australia, Michaelis imagines summer. He thinks of mulberry trees and bright sand and bare feet with soles toughened by heat-softened roads. But winter has another two months to go here. They won't be staying in Sydney, not even for a day. They are going straight to Newcastle. Rebecca and Brent have come to pick them up from the airport. Rebecca and Brent, whoever they are. Rebecca hugs Michaelis and holds him at arm's length.

'Gosh, you've grown,' she says.

Michaelis stands there stiffly and stares at her, feeling the awkwardness of his own smile. He doesn't say that he can't remember her. The only thing that he knows of Rebecca is that Mum used to get cassette tapes from her when they lived in Bergen op Zoom. On the tapes, you'd hear her talking about things, nothing in particular, just life back in Newcastle. Mum would listen to the tapes when she got sad and lonely.

'I can't wait to see what's changed in Newcastle,' Mum says.

'Not much,' Rebecca says. 'Still the same old place. Hasn't taken off quite yet.'

'But any moment,' Brent says. 'Any moment.'

Michaelis and Con walk to the beach as soon as they arrive at Rebecca and Brent's house. They are still wearing the clothes they wore when they got off the plane: jeans and long-sleeved checked shirts.

The beach has been gouged by storms. With each wave, a mountain of foam buries the length of the ocean baths. Then the sea draws back, and for a moment the water is too far away to be threatening. They start racing the waves. Michaelis follows Con and thinks that this is exactly when he is closest to his brother, behind him on some adventure, the silence between them broken only by a few spare words. They run along beside the pool, towards the edge of the rock shelf, as if they are going to jump into the water. Foamy dregs from the last wave recede around their feet. The water changes shape, gathers height and weight. They slow as the distance narrows.

'Run, Mike! Run, now!' Con turns on his heel and sprints back past.

Michaelis follows a step behind, always a step behind. The wave booms across the rocks. The roar gathers at his back. Spray climbs over his head. He feels pressure, a hum in the ground, finds a metal railing and clings with both arms. The water buries him.

There is such strength in the sea. He has forgotten it until now. It pulls at his limbs so that his feet touch nothing and only his desperate grip keeps him there. A sensation comes to him of being separate, of seeing it all from a great distance, as if he cannot reach out and touch the world. Then the noise dies in his ears; the sky appears again above him.

Michaelis walks home shivering in his wet jeans, with Con ahead, still dry, still composed. This was the same, not so long ago, in Bergen op Zoom, when the ice broke. A cold wind gusts around them along the broad, empty street. Merewether is full of such streets, no trees, the footpaths bare and exposed to the elements. In the summer, these roads sit under layers of heat and glare, and you long for a patch of shade as the sea evaporates from your skin, but it is hard to imagine now. They turn a corner, walk along a windswept park with the cricket oval dominating the centre, and there it is. Home.

The house sits facing the distant ocean against a dense tangle of lantana and saltbush and mulberry trees, halfway up a hill. They are staying in one room. They aren't paying rent, because they don't have much money. Dirk is repaying Rebecca and Brent by building a second level to the house. When the second level is built, they will live there.

Rebecca and Brent have a son who is Jonno's age. Mum met them at a mother's group, when they were living in Carrington. Rebecca's son is called Caleb and he throws tantrums all the time. He isn't allowed to watch cartoons because they are too violent and there are a whole bunch of foods that he isn't allowed to eat because they make him difficult to manage.

'She obviously doesn't understand,' Mum says to Dirk when Rebecca is out of earshot, 'what *really* makes children difficult to manage.'

The new school is not at all like the one he left behind in Bergen op Zoom. Like Carrington Public, you have to call everyone *Mr* or *Mrs* or *Sir*. There's another grey uniform, and there are lots of rules. The motto is *Manners Maketh Man*. His only friend is the librarian. Although he cannot speak English well, Michaelis picks up reading quickly. The librarian points him to the history books, and he reads about Alfred the Great, Caesar, William the Conqueror, Joan of Arc, Horatio Nelson. These are the people he gets to know in the language that is so clean in his head yet comes out so muddy from his mouth.

At home, Dirk is busy working above their heads every day. He seems to be building the house from his imagination. He is up there alone, his old scuffed tool belt around his waist, hammering and sawing, building the skeleton of a second storey against the vast sky with views all the way to the ocean.

'Your dad's a genius,' Brent tells Michaelis. 'You're lucky, son. You'll grow up knowing how to do whatever you want.'

Sometimes Michaelis sneaks up to have a look at Dirk's work when Dirk isn't around. One time he tripped over some wood while Dirk was there. His stepfather turned, his face all red and twisted up, and threw a spanner at Michaelis's head. Michaelis ducked and the spanner clattered against a wooden scaffold. Dirk picked up the spanner and went back to work, a grimace etched into his face, his shoulders knotted at his thick neck.

When he is not working, Dirk is teaching Mum to drive.

'It's not that hard!' He scowls at her. 'Why do you make everything so difficult? It's all in your head!'

Mum stalls the car and storms off a few times—once she stopped the car in the middle of the road and walked several kilometres to get home—but she keeps coming back.

Most days, Michaelis stays out of everyone's way. He finds a quiet corner and reads books or writes.

'It's not healthy,' Rebecca says to Mum, 'for a boy just to sit indoors by himself all day, just brooding like that.'

It is late July. Michaelis has a new book that Mum bought him for his tenth birthday, with a green leather cover, an illustrated version of *The Hobbit*, the title written in gold lettering on the front. The book is written in English, and he has written his name in English inside the front cover. But he gets the spelling wrong. Both his own name and Dirk's last name.

'Officially,' Mum tells him, 'you still have your father's last name, though you've never used it. But you could, if you wanted to.'

His real name is on the birth certificate that Mum has managed to carry around for years, but he doesn't want it. He doesn't want either of those names. From now on, wherever he is, here or back in Holland, he decides to call himself Michael.

Con and Michael get snorkelling gear for Christmas. They go to the ocean baths and snorkel in among the people. Tufts of seaweed wave from the bottom of the pool and crabs scuttle into cracks in the concrete. There are fish, small silver fish that are barely visible until they turn sideways to flit through the murky water between people's legs.

Beside the baths, where the water washes through rusted grates, a deep rock pool is connected by a narrow channel to the ocean. There are many more fish here, ones that look tropical: tiny yellow fish and others with black and white stripes. Con swears that an octopus inhabits the darkness of the rusted grate, but Michael's ears hurt when he goes down to look. He prefers staying near the top and running his hands along the crevices full of shells and fronds of weeds.

Next Con leads Michael onto the rock shelf from which the open ocean stretches, heaving and dark, towards the coal ships on the horizon. Con fixes the mask to his face and jumps into the open sea. His head bobs up and he spits water from his snorkel. He stares straight ahead and begins paddling. Michael watches him grow small. He wonders if he should follow, break through his own terror and jump into the ocean. Con stops and turns. Michael feels his body tense and gets ready. Con waves at him and shouts something. *Stay there.* Michael waves back, flushed with relief. Con disappears.

Not long after that, Con does some labouring work for the next-door neighbour and he uses what he earns to buy an aluminium hand spear with a three-pronged head. The first time he goes out, he comes back with two fish. He fillets them as if he's been doing it all his life and cooks them up for himself for lunch.

Michael and Mum watch him head out there some time after that. Con is tiny against the water. He's out much further than surfers, further even than the dolphins that cruise past the coast in the afternoons. He is not yet thirteen, but he does things that adults are afraid to do.

'I can't watch him do that,' Mum says. 'I don't know why he's so reckless. Sometimes I wonder if he wants to be alive at all.'

They move into the finished upper storey of the house and Michael shares a room with Con again, and Mum has laid down the usual straw tiles and put up some pictures that she painted herself. The cake Mum baked for her own birthday was left too long in the oven and collapsed into a hard shell. Dirk gave her a present and then drove off. Mum sits in her bedroom for a long time, wiping her eyes, and Con comes in and hands her a box all wrapped up. She undoes the wrapping and inspects the chocolates.

Her face drops. 'These aren't even good quality, Con! Why can't you at least give me *good* chocolate?'

Con storms out of the house. Mum begins crying even more, big wracking sobs. Michael is holding his own present: jade earrings he bought at the Mother's Day markets at the new school. They have made him repeat a year at school because of his bad English, but his teacher, Mrs Ross, offered to let him live with her if that would be easier on Mum. Mum was shocked. 'Why,' she asked, 'would anyone make such an offer?'

The earrings that Michael bought at the stall are antique and you have to screw them onto your ears very firmly like little vices to make them stay. He's holding the present in his hands, lingering in the doorway, watching Mum cry, wondering if he should give her the earrings. He decides to hold off.

Con is downstairs, at the back of the garden, sharpening the knife he uses to gut the fish he catches when he goes spearfishing: a filleting knife with a long, rusty blade. Only the edge is clean. He finishes sharpening the knife. He gets up and walks towards Michael with that blank look on his face, the knife loose in his hand.

He walks straight past without even a sideward glance, pulls his bag full of snorkelling gear onto his back and jumps on his bike. He vanishes down the sloping road, through the ripples of midday heat.

Later, he returns with three big, silvery fish, guts them out the back and throws the entrails in the bushes. Mum comes down to watch him.

'Con,' she says, placing a hand on his neck. 'How are you?'

'Good,' Con says.

'Really?'

'Really.'

'I'm so sorry about what I said. I didn't mean it at all. It was lovely of you to buy me chocolates. I mean, I do like quality, but it doesn't matter. It was a nice thought, really.'

'It's fine.' Con doesn't look up at her.

He scrapes his knife once more across the outer skin of the fish. Scales litter the ground at his feet. They glint on his fingers as he reaches into the splayed belly.

Mum straightens and stands beside him, folds her arms into her chest, a helpless expression on her face. 'I'm so sorry. About everything. Do you understand, Con? Do you understand?'

Con flashes a dazzling smile. 'Don't worry about it, Mum. I've already forgotten.'

She walks off. Con's face goes blank again as he throws the last of the entrails into the bushes. He stands there for a moment, his stained hands loose by his sides, then he turns to Michael.

'You know,' Con says, 'there's something about your face. It always makes me want to hit you.'

When Dirk comes home, Michael hears arguing—Mum sobbing, Dirk's voice low and fierce. Michael lies in bed, his body rigid. Outside he can hear crickets, a curtain of them through the night, and beyond that the ocean, the same as it has always been.

Nikki and Susan come to visit. They live in Queensland now, in Brisbane, not so far from Bribie Island. Nikki has an uncle in Newcastle and Michael spends an afternoon with him there. Nikki and Michael wander around Hamilton together, the old neighbourhood where they both once lived. Nikki is still the same gentle, quiet boy he used to be, although Michael finds that he is not as drawn to him as he once was. For the first time, he wonders if Nikki isn't a girl's name.

Susan gives them a dollar each and they walk down to a corner store together. They don't talk about why Michael has returned, or about Holland. It is easier to pretend that nothing has changed. Michael buys a packet of chips and eats without really tasting them. Nikki buys a packet of instant noodles and, when they get home, cooks them and shares them with Michael. Not long after that, he goes back to Queensland with his family.

And then it is time to leave Rebecca and Brent's house. They pile into their beat-up car, with a trailer full of stuff behind them. Mum and Rebecca hug.

'Be good,' Rebecca says.

Mum laughs and promises to call. The engine splutters into gear and they accelerate down the hill.

'Thank God that's over,' Mum says. 'I couldn't stand another minute with those people and their ridiculous ideas. They were happy to criticise me, but they call that raising a child?'

'They were *your* friends,' Dirk says.

'Things change. They always change.' She looks at Dirk when she says this, challenging him with her eyes, and then everyone in the car is silent.

Bar Beach is only the next suburb along, but it is as green and overgrown and damp with shade as Merewether's streets are barren and scoured by glare. Mum drives off every weekday to study nursing at university. Things will be better once they have two incomes, but Dirk is struggling to find enough work.

Their new house has two levels. The bottom level is below the street, and you can smell the rising damp. Perhaps it is the sea, which is not so far away. There are mining tunnels beneath the ground, their neighbour remarks. Everywhere, the ground is riddled with holes, long winding tunnels from the days when the ground under the city itself was mined for coal. You don't see it, but they're there, the tunnels.

All of this, all of the ground beneath their house and in the entire city, is a subsidence area, shifting by small degrees. Michael and Con have their bedroom downstairs, next to the kitchen. The concrete floor is covered in bright yellow straw tiles, just like the last house, and many before that, but Michael knows that each house is different. There is a window at street level, narrow and short. He can see the feet of people as they walk past.

Summer is drawing to a close, but you can't tell, not yet. The sea is warm and the days linger. The heat settles over everything and it is easier to forget things. Bergen op Zoom. No one here knows what that means. The words are beginning to sound strange on his tongue. They have not heard from or spoken of Dad for many, many months.

A friend of Mum's from university drops her off one day, a large man with a round face, a hunched posture and big glasses.

'This is Simon, boys.'

Simon smiles, shakes their hands, and his gaze drops to his feet. Simon is twenty and drives everywhere on a motorbike.

Dirk is out looking for work and will have to meet Simon some other time. Simon doesn't stay long. When he gets ready to leave, Mum goes out the front with him to say goodbye and does not come back for a while.

Later that day, Dirk is holding Mum against the wall, one hand crushing her neck, the other clenched into a fist.

'Fucking shut up!' Dirk tells her. '*Godverdomme!*'

Mum looks like nothing next to Dirk's bulk.

'Let her go,' Michael screams, 'or I'll call the police!'

Dirk looks down at him. It is as close to mounting a challenge as Michael has ever come, and no one is more surprised than Michael himself. Not a shred of bravura lingers in his body, but there is rage—helpless, frightened, focused rage that blazes from his face.

Dirk steps away from Mum. He gives the barest hint of a shrug, lifts and drops his hands, walks past Michael and stomps up the stairs. Mum touches Michael's head and walks past him too. Their bedroom door closes. The house fills with conversations Michael cannot hear.

That evening, Dirk comes down to their room and looks at Michael and Con. His eyes are red with grief, his cheeks wet. 'I'm leaving. Your mother doesn't want me.'

Michael has never seen Dirk cry before. It is the most shocking thing he has ever seen. 'When will you come back?'

'I don't know. Maybe never.'

'Don't go! Please don't.' The thought of Dirk going fills him with panic. Mum is so frail by herself.

Dirk wipes his nose and shrugs. 'Too late. Your mother doesn't love me. It's because of you.'

Before Michael can answer, Dirk is gone. The two

brothers lie in silence on the bunk. The front door opens and slams shut. Dirk's car rattles off down the street. Con begins to tap on the side of the bunk, a soft, complex rhythm that Michael has been listening to forever.

~

They live in Newcastle East now. Close to the sea, on the inner edge of the city, the part that juts out to form one arm of the harbour. The sea presses against this strip of land from three different directions, which you notice at night, when the murmur fills the air and haze drifts over everything. The houses huddle on a latticework of narrow, crisscrossing streets. No matter which direction the wind comes from, you can taste salt in the air. It seeps into stone and wood and fills metal with veins of rust.

Simon has started coming by their place a lot. He is large yet unobtrusive. He doesn't even raise his voice. Mum is happy. Michael can see her gums more when she smiles, like she is growing younger.

And it is strange how quickly he has become used to Dirk's absence. The terrace feels alive, with its narrow, creaking stairs and wooden windows that rattle on windy nights. The bedroom Con and Michael share has an enclosed balcony. The ageing terraces on the other side of the street are nearly the same as theirs, although they are all painted differently. Some have stained glass while others have wooden shutters, and Michael almost imagines that he could jump across, so narrow is the street, and the sounds of people talking or playing music in other houses come at him as if from another room.

Simon drops by one day, and stays for dinner. Michael, his legs crossed, his elbows on the table, watches Simon and Mum talking and laughing. Simon makes *him* laugh. Or lets him laugh, and it is strange not to feel afraid for once of the man in the house. To not have reason to, even if a part of you is watchful for the smallest changes.

Michael wakes up some mornings and feels a sense of doom like a weight on his chest. There is no explaining it, nothing obvious, but it is a belief that he has, a knowledge about the world. Bad things will come from nowhere, surging like the roots of fig trees through footpaths.

And that part of him drifts but never sleeps. Lying on the floor, with the night against the windows, upstairs in his bedroom, Michael listens to the tape player he got for Christmas. He owns one tape, the soundtrack to *Rocky III*. The night is still warm enough to wear a T-shirt, although he can feel the steady descent of the city into cooler weather, the edge to the air. Michael lies with his head against the stereo and listens to 'Eye of the Tiger'. In the middle of the song, he hears a loud banging. When he switches off the stereo, he hears only the usual sounds— the city, traffic, the ocean—and he thinks that he might have imagined it until the hammering starts again.

'Open the door! Open the fucking door! I'm going to kill you! Let me in so I can fucking kill you!'

It is Dirk's voice, full of rage.

Con's face appears in the doorway. *Hide*, Mike! Now!' He runs downstairs to Mum, to defend her.

Michael stares after him. Conan the Barbarian wouldn't be trying to hide at a time like this. He'd be there, downstairs with Con, doing what he could, laying his life on the line. But Michael can imagine the headlines: family massacred, one survivor. There always needs to be a survivor. He rolls under the bed. Dirk yells and beats on the door with what sounds like a hammer. There's murder in his voice, a sorrowful, desperate violence that makes the muscles around Michael's bladder tighten inwards. The door opens. Dirk's footsteps bend the wooden boards downstairs.

Mum's voice is rapid and pleading. 'No one's here. See?'

'*Godverdomme*, you think I'm an idiot?'

Back and forth their voices go. Stop, start, Dirk's voice rising and rising towards the first blow. From where Michael lies under the mattress, he sees only a sliver of doorway.

'I'm sorry, Dirk. I'm so, so sorry.'

Then the door slams shut. A car roars off. Michael gets out from under the bed and goes downstairs. Mum is hugging Con. When she sees Michael, she beckons to him. They all hug. No one says anything. Michael is sick with relief, and shame because he did not defend Mum when she needed him.

'Who wants hot chocolate?' she asks.

They sit in front of the television and drink their hot chocolate. Mum wanders off. On his way to the toilet, Michael overhears her talking on the phone.

'No, no,' she says into the phone, 'you did the right thing.'

'Hey, Mike,' Con says furtively when he walks back. 'Check this out.'

They go up the stairs into Mum's bedroom. There, shoved under the bed, are a pair of pants, a shirt, a belt and a pair of shoes.

'Look at that,' Con says, and Michael hears in his voice a sudden depth of feeling, pure contempt. 'Just look at it. Where does she get these guys from? This one even forgot his fucking clothes.'

~

The road lifts and the coastal suburbs spread through the back window of the car. Cliffs and hills rise up to the distant white finger of the Obelisk, the ocean lies over the trees and the houses, and everything is caught in the dazzling glare of the sun. And then comes the lurch as the road enters a steep decline, as if something of your insides is left behind, and you can never be prepared and the ocean is gone. Michael sits beside Mum in the front seat. Jonno sits in the back.

'Dirk has lost everything. Besides, how would I look

after Jonno right now? He isn't working and I am, so it just makes sense.'

Mum is explaining again why Jonno lives mainly with Dirk a few suburbs away, while Con and Michael stay with her. Michael doesn't know why she keeps explaining it. He really doesn't mind. Things have settled down since Dirk beat at the door with a crowbar. But there is a rippling through Michael's spine whenever they go to drop off Jonno, a sickly feeling that doesn't abate until the homeward stretch. Mum usually takes Con as well, but he's off spearfishing again.

Con has a spear gun now. On mornings when the wind comes from the right direction, he gets on his bike, bag strapped to his back, brimming with equipment, gun in one hand, and he silently pedals out of sight. He brings back huge fish with tiny holes behind their dark, foggy eyes where the spear went in. Sometimes he talks about seeing sharks out there. Once he even tried to feed them.

'Here we are,' Mum murmurs.

She pulls into the driveway. Dirk comes out to meet them, pale belly hanging over his jeans, hair oily and dishevelled. He runs one hand through his beard and waits. Mum gets out of the car and unstraps Jonno from the back. Michael climbs out last, extracting his limbs from the front seat as if he doesn't quite know what to do with them. His joints have been clicking and aching of late, particularly his knees, which he notices more when he lies on the bottom bunk of the bed that he still shares with Con. Growing pains, Mum calls them.

'Hi, Dirk. How are you?'

Without answering, Dirk takes Jonno. Mum waits and stares up at his face. Her face is level with the dark jut of his beard. They stand there in silence, like the shimmering mirage of a family. Michael licks his lips and looks across at the bleak house behind them, the three-storey housing commission block beyond.

'Well, we had a nice time,' Mum says.

Dirk gives a short nod of his head. Michael puts his hands in the pockets of his jeans and moves closer to Mum. Dirk's eyes move across Michael without any recognition.

'Your birthday's coming up,' Dirk says at last, looking at Mum.

'Yes.'

'Here.'

Dirk gives her something all wrapped up. Mum takes it, undoes the carefully tied ribbon and peels away the crepe paper to reveal a white marble elephant the size of her hand.

She looks caught off balance. 'That's very nice of you, Dirk. It's really...really lovely.'

Dirk doesn't move. 'For luck. The last thing you'll ever get from me.'

Something shifts in Mum's face. 'Well, thank you. We'd better go.' She gives Jonno a hug and a kiss. Her hand stays on his cheek for a moment, then she turns away. 'Bye then, Dirk.'

They get back into the car.

'He can give such nice gifts,' Mum says as the car door closes.

She bites her bottom lip tightly until a sob escapes. She drops the elephant behind her seat with a sigh and a rustle of crepe paper, rattles the keys, scrapes them against the ignition and presses the clutch.

'Stupid bastard. He gives such good gifts and always finds a way to ruin them!'

Michael looks towards Jonno, standing there waving as they back out of the drive. Jonno is three, a thin, blond-haired boy. Sometimes Michael feels affection for him and sometimes he is the enemy. But when he smiles, he reveals his gums like Mum, and he smiles now and waves wildly at Michael and Mum in the car. Michael waves back.

Dirk stands behind Jonno, arms at his sides, his eyes darkened by the weight of his forehead. Mum pulls out onto the street, up the hill. When they reach the crest, Michael sees the sea and the tension tumbles from his chest.

Mum wipes her eyes with the back of her hand. 'It's hard. It's too hard.'

She shakes her head. They keep on driving.

The following week, when they go to pick up Jonno, Dirk isn't waiting for them out the front. When they knock on the door, he doesn't answer. Michael peers through the window; his breath fogs against the glass. He looks back at Mum and no words come into his mouth.

Something rises in Mum's voice. 'What? What is it?'

'I don't know.'

She puts her hand on his shoulder. 'What? Don't just stand there. Let me see.'

He stands beside Mum as she presses her face against the glass.

'It's empty.' Mum tries the front door and it is open. What little furniture Dirk possessed is gone. The place smells of detergent and the carpet is tacky underfoot. Sunlight pours through flimsy white lace curtains. Mum walks from one end of the house to the other without saying a word. There is a note under a stone on the kitchen counter. Mum reads it, crumples the paper, throws it to the ground. Michael picks it up. There aren't many words on it:

> *I've taken Jonno away from here. You'll never see*
> *him again. Come after us and I'll kill us both.*

~

From Mum's bedroom window Michael can see the back fence over which Simon jumped that night in nothing but his underpants. This part of the town has an older feel, a bit like Europe—the sprawling cathedral above the mall, like something medieval, the ruins of Fort Scratchley on the headland, with cannons that once fired on Japanese submarines. Near the remains of the fort is the breakwall and above it the lighthouse. Back from this extend the narrow streets and century-old terraces ravaged by salt. Past that, hidden on the top of a hill, is the school where he first went as a boy six years ago, when he didn't know a word of English, walking with Mum towards the sky through the corridor of figs.

It is never entirely still in this part of town. The fountain built into the nearby park is always alive, the five roaring columns of water much higher than a boy or even a man, and twice as wide. The columns take turns to rise to their full height and then recede and bubble away into the dark-tiled circular surface set into the grass. After he has gone swimming alone, he steps from grate to grate and waits for the water columns to rise and hide him from the world.

Across the park, looking out over Newcastle Beach at the end of a busy mall, sits the hospital. At night, it is all lit up, endless rows of narrow windows. Mum will work there when she has finished her studies. There is a brothel in an old wooden terrace around the corner in Zaara Street, with the solitary red light that goes on at night. That means, Con tells him, that they are open for business—he knows because he checked. Down another narrow street, all the way to the end, between two rows of old terraces, on a patch of grass, stands a lonely bench, and there are often needles lying around, or broken beer bottles. Beyond the bench, a cliff drops to the ocean. The baths are there, carved out of stone, the headland to one side, and an inlet directly below composed of rock and seaweed and restless currents, facing the container ships on the horizon. Michael sits there some mornings, staring over the sea and watching the first swimmers, most of them white-haired locals, gather for their daily ritual. The tones of their conversations drift up to him.

Gezellig.

When he gets home, no one asks where he has been. Mum's grief fills the house. She has hired a private detective to track down Jonno—she is too afraid to call the police—but a month has passed and there isn't any news. Late at night, Michael hears her crying: long, soft sobs muffled by closed doors and the noises of the city. He falls asleep and awakes with the sea pressing against his ears, and for a moment there is nothing else.

He can hear another voice sometimes in the bedroom with Mum. Simon returned after that night and not a word was spoken about what had happened. More of his things turned up around the house. He started staying longer. Now it's as if Simon has always been living there. Despite her grief, Mum studies with Simon every day. They sit side by side in exams and she copies his answers. They go halves with the shopping and the rent, although Mum is the one who keeps the house tidy and cooks dinner.

Soon Mum will be moving them again, to another place, with a garage, so that Simon has somewhere to put his motorbike. On weekends, Simon and Mum ride together, across the harbour, to work at the mental hospital.

Mum sometimes says that she could never make it through this terrible time without Simon's support and that they should be happy for her that she's found someone. She's really talking only to Con. He looks at her, gives a shrug, and something hard and grey creeps into his gaze. Con doesn't dwell on many things, but he remembers weakness.

They went spearfishing together one day, Con and Simon, while Michael watched from the shore. After a couple of hours, Con emerged from the water carrying half a dozen fish longer than his forearm and glistening fat, each with a tiny, precise hole behind the eye, while Simon had caught nothing. They stood near one another and did not say anything.

'I don't know how you do it,' Simon said finally, shaking his head.

Con is nearly as tall as Simon, but leaner, more evenly proportioned. He showed his teeth for the briefest moment, then went off to a separate spot to gut the fish.

Michael wakes in the middle of the night. On his way to the outside toilet, he finds Mum sitting on a step in the darkness of the stone courtyard, smoking a cigarette. He sits down beside her. A few stars glimmer through the air blown in from the factories and the orange glow thrown up by the city lights. A train gathers pace in the distance as it leaves Newcastle Station.

'It's such a lonely sound,' she says.

'What?'

'The waves. Those waves just crashing against the shore. It's so...*restless*. I just wish that it would *stop* for a little while.'

'I like it. I love it.'

Mum lights up another cigarette and stares at the tip. 'I used to dream about it back in Holland, yearn for it, you know? Now I think I never want to hear it again. Strange how it seems to get louder at night. There is nothing kind in that sound. Just motion, endless motion. It sounds like loss.'

'It's just the sea.'

'I'll never forgive myself for abandoning Jon.'

'But you didn't. Dirk stole him.'

'In the end it doesn't make any difference.'

'We'll find him, Mum.' Michael does his best to sound reassuring, to speak to her in the way that Simon speaks to her. 'We'll find him.'

He puts a hand on her shoulder and notices how his arm is level when he does so, and it is strange to think that he is as tall as her now, and that he will keep on growing.

She glances at him. 'Do you think it was worth it?'

'What?'

'Leaving Dirk.'

'Yes.'

'Do you miss Holland?'

Michael nods and feels something tighten in his throat.

'What do you miss about it?'

'Lots. I wish that I could go back. I don't know if I want to see Dad again. I think about him, though.'

'Every decision has a cost, one way or another,' Mum murmurs. Stars slip across the sky and the fence swallows them one by one. 'It was a different world back there,' she goes on. 'When I left your father, your grandmother made me see a priest. I rode on my bike to see him in the next village. I told the priest about what your father had done to Con. It was so hard to say those things. The priest said that I probably wasn't satisfying him properly as a wife. I couldn't get out of there fast enough. I knocked over the chair and cycled home in tears. My mother was furious at me for embarrassing her in front of a priest. That was always her biggest worry, being embarrassed. She's more afraid of that than dying.'

'I hope she does die.'

'She'll live a long time. Even if I didn't love her, she'd be there inside my heart.'

Michael understands. Dirk still haunts him like that. But Dirk is gone. And Dad is on the other side of the world. The memory of his father is once more growing dull.

'You look like him, you know.' She is watching him in the darkness.

'Who?'

'Andreas. You look more like him than Con does. You shouldn't be so shocked. Andreas was a very handsome man. You never knew him when he was young. That's more what you look like—him when he was young. Yes, you should have seen him.'

Something has come into her eyes. She walks every evening along the beach with Simon. They hold hands. They talk for hours in bed at night. But Michael never sees that look in Mum's eyes when she speaks about Simon. Perhaps it is because she's already had to start forgetting important parts of him, the way he jumped over their fence that night.

'Do you still love him?'

Mum hesitates. 'Who? Andreas? No. Maybe a part of me does. It's more pity, I think. And anger. I could have been happy with him. But it doesn't matter. It's not important. At some point, we really have to be *here*.'

Michael smiles at her. He sits on the step, arms wrapped around his knees, hunched into himself. It is peaceful right now, except for the sound of the ocean rolling over every stone surface. He thinks of how the sea touches the other side of the world too, where so many of his memories and questions remain. You get used to it, the waves breaking on the shore, and the wind and the noises caught up within. And when you do, you can imagine, if only for a while, that there is no sound at all.

NEWCASTLE

8

'He's here,' Con said.

The car pulled into the driveway and we made our way down the stairs. I wasn't sure whether to be happy or excited. I felt curious more than anything else. I had no idea what Con was thinking—I could never tell from the look on his face.

Con and I stood out the front of the house. The car came to a halt. It was a hot afternoon, the beginning of a school holiday in spring. There was no wind. Patches of harbour shimmered between the buildings off to one side.

We had moved to this part of the city recently with my mother and Simon. Our latest home was the top level of an old two-storey brick house overlooking the mall. From the windows of our living room you could see Stockton Beach, its dark fleck of a shipwreck marking the sand in the distance. Inside, the usual straw tiles covered dirty carpet. A fresh straw odour still filled every space. At one end, Con and I shared a bedroom, as we had for most of our childhoods, but we never would again after this. Soon my mother and Simon would buy a weatherboard cottage in Islington, near the industrial part of the harbour. My mother would no longer put down straw tiles and instead rip up the carpet and polish the wood underneath. When I moved next, it would be on my own. But that was still years away.

My mother got out of the car first, her make-up messy, a complicated smile on her face. She opened the back door. There was a pause. Then a boy emerged and looked shyly in our direction. He was six years old, tall for his age, and lanky with light-coloured skin. His hair was a luminous blond. His strong forehead ended in eyebrows etching towards one another, and underneath that a fierce blue gaze. He already had a prominent chin, a broad nose and a mouth that locked into a compact sort of smile, though his lips were soft, and shaped, I realised, like our mother's.

'He's turned into a little man,' Con said.

I didn't say anything. Apart from that honeyed blaze of hair, Jonno immediately reminded me of his father, the man who had abducted him and vanished into Queensland three years earlier.

Con stepped close and ruffled his hair. 'Jonno,' he said with much greater warmth and affection than I'd heard in his voice for a long time. 'Hey, Jonno.'

'Hug your brother,' my mother said, looking at me. And I did.

Jonno stayed for a week. Con took him rock fishing. They went out for a day, and I knew what Jonno was in for, the wind and the salt and the sun and the endless search for the perfect spot, and Con's gaze always somewhere up ahead, until he caught the fish and gutted them on some rock.

When it was my turn, I took him to the movies. We lived near the cinema, part way along the hill that rose up to the cathedral. Jonno and I walked down to the cinema together. We were companionable enough, but we had little to say to one another. We did not talk about his father or about the three years that had passed since Dirk had disappeared with him. He answered my questions economically. He did not ask any of his own. We watched the movie, and walked back in silence.

Although I admitted this to no one, the truth was that I had not missed Jonno. He had left no gaping hole in my existence. I'd been affected by our mother's grief at his disappearance, but not by my own. I had been too relieved when Dirk left—too absorbed in my own life, in pulling myself out of the gloom, in trying to get my stepfather out of my system. At school, the other children and teachers didn't even know that I had a younger brother.

They did not know about my stepfather either, though I would have nightmares about him and still had the habit of second-guessing the simplest movements of my body, as if he might emerge from nowhere to pick me up by the hair or give me an open-handed slap across the face. *Een klap.*

Jonno didn't stay with us long. Soon my mother was driving him back to the airport, to the plane that would carry him to Dirk, in Queensland. While he had been with us, our mother had been elevated by nervous energy. But when she came home without him, she went into her room, closed the door and cried until it was dark outside.

She said that Jonno had cried too, when he was away from Con and me, when he was out of our sight. His reserve had collapsed at the airport, in departures, when the reality of leaving set in. He had not let go of our mother for a long time.

'You'll see us again soon,' she told him.

Jonno's visits took place in holiday periods, four per year. Our mother always launched into these times with a tense, forced gaiety—she was determined to make a good *holiday* for Jonno and for all of us, as a family. Fights happened more easily. Our mother and Simon would argue more.

I could see the tension building in her before Jonno arrived, as she went through all the details and paid for the tickets, and then the fervour with which she threw herself into cooking and planning and observing, constantly observing—to make sure that he was at least having a good time when he was there with us, that we were all functioning as a family should.

A year after we started seeing Jonno again, when I was fourteen, an earthquake hit Newcastle. Buildings collapsed all over the city, people died, foundations cracked. The mall alongside the harbour withered. The hospital overlooking the sea split down to its core and decayed over the following years into a shell. A new hospital opened somewhere else inland. Eventually most of the shell was demolished and what remained was converted into luxury apartments. The old hospital is long gone now, and you would never know that this was the place where, decades ago, Jonno had been born.

By the time the earthquake struck, we had left our house above the mall, the house from which it was possible to see the distant wreck of the *Sygna* and the wilderness that hid the airport where Jonno departed and arrived. Our mother and Simon had bought the cottage in Islington and began to renovate it. Con and I were given separate rooms, but whenever Jonno came, he stayed in mine, because we were closer in age.

Jonno wanted the door open at night. And he wanted the light on in the corridor outside. I let him keep the door open, but I wasn't happy about it. At his age, I'd been terrified of the dark. His father had made few allowances for me.

Unlike Con, who always slept without even seeming to breathe, as if he'd abandoned his body, Jonno was a restless sleeper. He was much noisier asleep than awake. I'd constantly hear the creak and racket of the mattress springs, the snoring and grunting, and the way that he cried out, struggling against things I couldn't see. He moaned a lot, deep in his throat, and ground his teeth. Sleep seemed to be one long nightmare for him.

I still slept in the bunks that my brother and I had once shared, and they were mine to do with as I pleased. I'd pulled the bottom bunk out at a right angle to have a clear view of the ceiling.

I insisted that Jonno sleep on the top, although I knew the bottom was better for him. He often fell out of bed and usually clambered back up without complaint. Some nights, though, I would wake to a heavy thump and see him sprawled unmoving in the shadows on the floor. I'd go back to sleep without bothering to wake him.

Once, I came out of a dream to see him falling from his bed, floating down towards me through the moonlight, his slack limbs spread, like he was offering me an embrace. Without thinking, I lifted my feet, planted them in his stomach and guided him over my head to the floor. My timing must have been perfect—I hardly felt him at all—and I easily fell back into sleep. When I woke up in the morning, he was still there, on the floor, beside my bed.

148

I didn't feel sorry for him. When he wasn't around, I barely gave him any thought at all. But I hated the effect Jonno had on my mother, on everyone, the way all that pain reared up in his wake, like stitches torn from a wound. I sometimes wished that she'd never hired the private detective to track Jonno down, that she'd left him out there as part of some sort of inevitable loss.

'He's your brother,' our mother would say. 'Don't ever forget that. This family has to stick together.'

Most of the history that Con and I shared was separate from Jonno. His life had begun much later than ours. He did not see what Dirk had been like to us, nor did he understand the things that bound Con and I together. We could never have explained it to Jonno. We did not get along most of the time, Con and I, but there was a connection between us as impenetrable to outsiders as a foreign language. When we joked about Dirk, Jonno would not say anything.

'Ah, good old Dirk,' my brother would remark, slapping me on the shoulder. 'Don't you miss him? Remember how he used to throw spanners at us? He taught us everything we know about getting out of the way!'

'And running.' I pictured Dirk, a nail-riddled plank raised in his hand, cursing as he pursued Con down the street.

Verdomme.

The three of us rarely did activities together, but Con sometimes played cricket with us in the backyard, mocking the way I threw the ball while smoothly encouraging Jonno. Con always seemed like a natural-born father to me, maybe because I had to work so hard for his approval. Jonno laughed softly at his jokes, which usually came at my expense, or made his own sparse comments towards me in an instinctive echo of Dirk's derisive humour. A shapeless dread would tug at my stomach when he did that, and Jonno became better at that commentary with each visit.

It was only much later that I started wondering about the life that Jonno led during those early years, the way that it must have unfolded for him after Dirk disappeared with him. A boy, not yet three years old, on a road trip with his father. I can only imagine the small, childish conversations he might have had with Dirk on that long drive into Queensland, away from the rest of us, and the days and weeks that followed, when it became clear he wouldn't be returning. Did he cry? Did his father call this weakness? I wonder whether Dirk ever offered him comfort.

In Queensland, with the threat of murder–suicide covering his tracks, Dirk set about making a new life. He abandoned carpentry and began a degree in computing. He became a sought-after expert in information technology. Jonno spent a lot of his childhood alone. As he grew up in some Brisbane outer suburb, he learned to wash his own clothes and prepare his own food and entertain himself. He ate a lot, but he didn't eat well— not like we did with our mother's cooking. He wandered back and forth through his father's house and watched a lot of television. He never told me more about his childhood than that.

But in the hidden months between those visits that punctuated my adolescence, he started to grow much larger than other children. He gathered weight, so that each time I saw him, the change was more obvious; he filled more of the space between us. I don't know the exact point when he became stronger than me. And in the departures lounge, after a few years, to my mother's disquiet, he no longer cried when it was time to say goodbye. I have always felt the two were connected.

'Seeing any girls?' Con asks as we sit in the back of our mother's Torana.

'No,' Jonno answers.

'Come on,' Con says with a wink and a winning flash of his teeth. 'A handsome kid like you. Bet there've been a few girls. Are you holding out on me, your own brother?'

A blush creeps into Jonno's cheeks, and he stares out the window. But when he glances back, his eyes reveal nothing. Jonno is ten. Con is twenty. He is a man, and I am somewhere in between.

It's unbearably hot in the car. Con and I are shirtless, in our board shorts. Jonno is wearing baggy board shorts in a man's size and two huge T-shirts that are stained under the armpits. We are going to the beach, and I know that he won't take those shirts off, even when he goes in the water. Our knees are all pressed into one another. Jonno's breath fills the back seat. His thighs are nearly as wide as mine.

'Make sure you date a *Greek* girl,' Con says, changing his voice, catching my eye, and I laugh.

By the time Jonno was seventeen, he reminded me of a giant in a story I'd once read, who grew so large that in the end only the sea would support his weight.

Gradually, it became harder for him to move. He started having to think about what chair he needed to sit in. The front passenger seat of any car became his without discussion, and the car would sag as he got in. Our mother worried about his weight but didn't want to deny him the things that she had always given to us. Con and I hardly mentioned Jonno's weight either, although it was always there, the thought of it, its practical application. By this time, he had stopped going fishing or snorkelling with Con, or to the movies with me.

Con and I would walk down the street and he'd come behind at a glacial pace. People turned sometimes to watch him pass. Con and I were always thinking and talking and obsessing about women, while he said nothing.

By the time he was a man, his thighs were as thick as my waist. When he travelled by plane, he booked two seats. When I stood beside him, I was reminded of how I used to feel around his father as a boy, insubstantial and light, like I might be blown away or broken by a stiff wind. Jonno's immense size made me feel as if, despite all of those years, I had not grown up at all.

But he was the first and only baby I'd ever held in my arms. I was seven. He was feather-light, as if the breeze might lift him, and bald as a Buddhist monk. As he learned to crawl and walk and form his first words, I remember how Dirk treated him differently. He never laid a hand on him, never raised his voice, never mocked him, but then I cannot forget that when Dirk disappeared into Queensland, it was Jonno that he abducted and threatened to kill, not me.

When Jonno was a boy, I grabbed him once by the arm and punched as hard as I could, in the meat of his bicep. He had touched my things and broken something. He stared at me, his blue eyes unwavering, and ran off.

When he was twenty-one he towered over me. We

were standing together, waiting to go somewhere with our mother. I grabbed his hands in a playful imitation of wrestling. He applied an excruciating pressure and forced me to my knees. My wrists felt like twigs. His face, buried in the placid roundness of the fat, was marked by a slight smile, the eyes elsewhere, as if he didn't know the strength in his grip.

But when Jonno was a toddler, I used to lie in bed and fantasise about stabbing his father to death. I loved to go into the mad, thrusting detail, the ransacking of my knife into Dirk's belly, the simple, honest labour of cutting off his head and throwing it down the stairs (my satisfaction in the dense, fleshy thud), clapping my hands, turning to our mother and saying, 'There, it's over.'

As an adult, I have spoken to Dirk briefly a few times on the phone.

'Hello,' he says.

'Hello, it's Michael.' I hesitate. 'Is Jon there?'

'No,' Dirk says in a voice that is deeper than Jonno's but not all that different. He is courteous and contained, as if we have never met in person. He doesn't say my name. 'I'll get him to call you back.'

'Thanks,' I tell him.

I put down the phone and notice the tightness in my lungs. The way my heart has decided to change its movement.

Is that all?

When I was thirty, Dirk drove Jonno to Newcastle to the house that I shared with my first wife and our newly born daughter. Dirk did not come in; he dropped Jonno nearby, then drove the car alongside the house very slowly before accelerating away down the street. Jonno and I stood there staring after him in silence.

'That,' Jonno said, 'is just his idea of a joke.'

Dirk stayed somewhere else in the city, in a hotel, but he had a camera, and, like a tourist, he visited the old suburbs in which we had once lived as a troubled family: Newcastle East, Hamilton, Carrington. I don't know what he was looking for in those places. But I have gone back there, too.

The first day Jonno stayed in my house, he sat on the sofa and stared down at my daughter over massive folded arms. His heels flung before him were like cracked stone. He had sores around his toes and ankles, sores that must have been caused by lack of circulation and the simple pressure of moving and supporting that weight. But after he had relaxed, he picked up my daughter a few times and lifted her to his gaze. She was calm in his hands, in the cradle of his fingers that were the width of her wrists. My daughter was fascinated by Jonno's largeness, his implacable patience, the distantly amused intelligence in his eyes.

Jonno stayed at my house a few days, and then met his father somewhere else in the city and they drove back to Queensland. I can see the two of them in that car, filling the front of it with their breath and their bulk, re-enacting an older journey.

After that, we talked mainly on the phone. We didn't talk much about Jonno's personal life. The closest we came was when we talked about his studies or the mother we tenuously shared, both of us holding a part that did not quite join. Mainly Jonno told me about movies or television shows that he had watched. He was an expert on every series out of America, and could discuss swathes of animation from Japan. He spoke of these things with breathy authority.

He stayed up late into the nights. He didn't need much sleep, he said. For a while he tried to lose weight by holding one side of a Hills hoist out in the backyard of his father's house and walking around and around in circles.

It makes me think of how I too spent a lot of time alone as a boy, always in motion, wandering aimlessly, losing myself in one way or another. I walked everywhere across Newcastle. I have a clear memory of walking once along the expanse of Bar Beach car park. I was fourteen. It was bright, sunny. The car park was like an enormous shovel tilted and poised above the sea. I walked to the edge of the cliff and stared out at the water. Someone called out to me. I turned. A man was running towards me, his face a mask of alarm.

'Did you feel that?' he asked. 'Are you okay?'

'Feel what?' I asked.

This was the earthquake in 1989 that did so much damage in the city. That is my memory of it: that I did not feel it at all.

Years later—after she broke up with Simon, and after Con and I both moved out and started on our separate lives— my mother moved closer to Jonno, not to Brisbane but to the Gold Coast, which perhaps offered both proximity to Jonno and distance from Dirk. Jonno would come to visit her then on weekends, and Con and I would catch up with him once or twice a year.

My mother fell into a relationship with an older man. He would provide unwanted fatherly advice to the three of us whenever we came near. There was something obvious and absurd in his advice. To Jonno, it was about losing weight, about getting a grip on his life and showing some ambition. Brian was the former principal of a religious high school.

To my mother, Brian said once, 'I really admire the fact that you can walk down the street with that boy without feeling ashamed.'

I never liked Brian, felt amazed that my mother could stay with him for so long and put up with his endless lecturing and demands. To Jonno, he was nothing, a drop of water off his back.

'I don't listen to him,' Jonno said. 'It's easy. You smile

and nod and you say as little as possible, and then he's happy.'

When he said that, it made me realise something. 'Do you do that with everyone?'

Jonno laughed.

I sometimes imagine antidepressants stored in his fat. I have not seen him angry or sad, not since he was a boy. I have never seen him ecstatic, either. I have never seen him shout in rage or curse or break into a run or hammer his fist against a table. Even as a man, he sounds, with that soft, high-pitched voice, like a boy.

'I don't want my children to die before me,' my mother would say when the pressure Jonno's heart was sustaining became clear: the vast, useless distances his blood had to be pushed—through hundreds and hundreds of kilometres of capillaries—to maintain his bulk.

A heart can be moved from one body to another and it will carry on as if it doesn't know the difference. At the thinnest point, its walls are only a few millimetres thick, yet it can beat for over a hundred years. For all of its size, Jonno's heart will probably not beat for anywhere near that time; it will likely just stop, the way a storm drops off in an instant, and the last laboured breath will leave my brother's chest. But that won't be the whole story.

We hardly talk now. Each phone conversation is like a troubled engine threatening to stall on the slightest incline. I speak more to my memories of Jonno than I do to him.

I do see him sometimes, though—or perhaps *see* is not the right word. Rather I find myself daydreaming, lost in the past, trying to imagine all the parts I don't know. Because when Jonno was out of sight for me as a boy, he didn't exist. But right now I am looking through *his* eyes as he walks with the other passengers towards a waiting plane.

He has just spent a holiday with us. Departures is left behind, and it is ahead of him too. He is six and used to travel already, like his brothers. Although he is slim, the tangle of weight and distance is beginning to form inside him. Our mother's smile is on his lips. He moves between worlds that change when he is not there. He is walking towards the plane that will carry him away again, from the life of our family to the quiet of his father's house.

9

Dutch is an awkward language. It sounds humorous to me even now, except when someone uses it in anger. When my stepfather cursed, I imagined dirt in his lungs, old black farming earth from the north of Holland, clotted with blood and bone.

Godverdomme.

Upstairs, in my room, Con is laying into me, and usually when he does this I keep quiet, play dead, wait for it to finish. But today I scream. My brother keeps going, one blow after the other, although bitter resignation kinks his closed mouth. He sees this as a betrayal. Through my screaming, I hear the creak of the stairs, our stepfather's heavy breath and his deep, guttural curses.

The door swings open. Dirk fills the doorway and my brother backs away. My brother is particularly handsome at times like this, upright, very alert. He doesn't show fear, not like I do.

Dirk moves between us, and his head swings from Con to me and back again. 'What did I tell you? *Idioot!*'

From where I sit on the floor, I can see the crack of his arse, huge and pale, with a swirl of black hair plunging into his corduroy pants. He wrenches off a paint-stained workboot and lifts it over his head. My brother throws a hateful glance my way before Dirk's back obscures him.

I wish that I could take satisfaction in what happens next, enjoy my brother's punishment. But I am waiting for my turn with Dirk. I am always second in line. With each lift of that boot, I glimpse my future.

Now, thirty years later, whenever I hear the word 'anticipation', or try to imagine what will happen next in my life, that feeling laps up against me, although my stepfather is nowhere in sight.

~

Metal chains squeal in protest with each thrust of my arms. My daughter is two, and she has learned to say 'more' and 'push' and 'harder'. With these three words, she keeps me busy. I push her on the swing and she keeps returning to me, hair floating on the air like an afterthought, a determined line in her jaw when she casts me a quick glance to make sure I won't give up.

This is one of the things we do together, this going to the park. Half of every week I take care of my daughter and we wander around the city looking for things to do. The other half of my daughter's week belongs to my wife. We are not divorced, we live in the same house, but our lives are neatly separated all the same. There are times when we do things together as a family, visits to the beach or the park or some other outing, and my wife always says, 'This is good, isn't it?' and I agree although my eyes don't. My eyes have always betrayed me, my emotions thrown up like moths trapped inside a lantern. But I have learned to look away at the crucial moments. I have learned that it is possible to do this with an entire life.

The time that my wife and I spend alone together happens after May is asleep, when we sit in front of the television. We massage each other's shoulders with oil for lovers and exchange conversation in the advertising spaces that dismember the usual television programs about crime and death. I don't mind talking then, because we are staring in the same direction. I have come to see television as one of the sacrifices you make for love.

After the park, I take May to the library. We walk in through the large, open doors just as a young woman walks out. She is wearing those tight pants that look like painted-on jeans. My gaze snags on her and I glance over my shoulder as she walks off.

Whenever such longing comes, I think of my real father, who was known for his wandering eye, and how he was generally forgiven for it because of his charming nature. I know more of my father through what my mother has given me than through my own interactions with him. He still lives in another country, on the other side of the world, and the last that I heard, he was caring for his other ex-wife, the religious one, who was dying of lung cancer. We haven't spoken in twenty years, but information trickles through.

'It's strange,' my mother will tell me, 'how you hardly saw him, but then you laugh or move your hand, just like that, and I can see him there, just like when I fell in love with him.'

This is the story I have of how my parents fell in love: my father was dating my mother's best friend. He was always talking to my mother whenever her friend was out of the room—a brush of his hand, a smile, playful and light, as if they were brother and sister. One day, he hugged his girlfriend, stared lingeringly at my mother and winked, like they were sharing a joke.

A year later, my brother was born, and three years after that I came along, a home birth on the thirteenth floor of an apartment block in a town near the southern border of Holland. My first words were Dutch, but I can't remember them.

I arrived early by kicking a hole in my mother's stomach; so I believed as a boy. I was always accused of a terrible clumsiness, and this version of events made sense to me. The midwife coughed and smoked through the whole labour and had to wipe the ash from my face before she announced, in a voice dry as paper, that I was the handsomest baby she'd ever laid eyes on. When my father returned from whatever errands had been absorbing him, he borrowed money from my grandfather for a bunch of flowers, came into the bedroom with the flowers in one fist, the other in his pocket, and stared at me long and hard.

'Are you sure that I'm the father?' he asked.

We moved on from Holland to England and rented an apartment where everything was coin-operated: the heating, the stove, the shower, the phone. We didn't have a lot of coins. My father was struggling to find work. He had borrowed five thousand guilders from my grandparents, but most of that money had vanished. There was a mystery to this money that I would hear of years later, yet what I grew up knowing was that we didn't have anything; that it caused the inevitable conflicts; that I would often turn blue with cold; that the walls ran with condensation; that my father was not often around; that I was not a good sleeper. My mother would walk the streets of London by herself, driven by loneliness and the crying that leaked out of me as if I were connected to some limitless reservoir beneath the city. 'The moment that I saw you,' my mother said, 'I knew that you had been here before, that you were an old soul.'

I think that my mother sometimes confuses unhappiness with experience.

~

May is in front of me, singing a song, completely lost in the moment. Sometimes she wakes me up like that, at five in the morning, singing in her bed, clapping her hands to mark the rhythm. I lift a finger to my mouth and catch her eye, and she smiles until she gets my meaning, then frowns and falls silent before running ahead into the open, quiet spaces of the library. I wonder suddenly if I am discouraging her zest for life. I imagine sometimes that I am moving through life like some kind of blundering surgeon, pinching off possibilities like they're arteries.

May wanders into the children's section and fondles the spines of books. She pulls the books out and leaves them splayed in her wake. Someone ought to pull her into line. I take a book about the decline of the Roman Empire from a shelf and sink into a chair. My daughter comes up to me and touches my knee.

'Done poo poo,' she tells me.

We collect our things and go to the toilet. I use up half a packet of wipes. Her underwear goes into the bin. My daughter stands on the counter next to the sink, sees herself in the mirror and starts swaying her hips from side to side, humming under her breath. I tell her to stop, and she puts more sideways thrust into her hips.

'Just cut it *out*,' I tell her in a sharper tone. She stops.

I regret it immediately. My daughter is not afraid of my wife's anger, only of mine. I get irritable when I am tired, and these days I am tired all the time. I have lost control of what I had always assumed would be mine: sleep. I knew that it was coming—plenty of people warned me—I just didn't know how *bad* that lack would be. My daughter wakes sometimes in the middle of the night crying so fiercely that her face develops a rash, and in that hysteria, she is impossible to communicate with. She looks enraged, as if she does not recognise a thing in this world. My wife, who gets up exactly half the time with her, holds her and rocks her and pleads and eventually starts crying herself. Please go back to sleep, she tells our daughter. Please, please, please go back to sleep. This can go on for hours. I just listen. The muscles in my arse are like the workings of a clock, marking the passage of this time by winding more tightly into themselves.

When it is my turn, I pick my daughter up and I also tell her to stop. If this doesn't work, I take her to the shower and hold her head near a stream of cold water and threaten to put her under. Twice I have put her head under. When I make this threat, she bites at her own sobs until they retreat back into her chest. Sometimes I imagine my daughter, twenty years from now, shrugging when someone asks about her overwhelming fear of water. I hold her after she has calmed down, until she goes to sleep, and feel tender at her peacefulness, her vulnerability. But I am ashamed rather than satisfied, and my wife treats me with a wounded contempt that transmits itself in the angle of her body, turned away from me in the bed.

With my daughter asleep, I lie down beside my wife, separated from the comfort layer of the mattress by the knots in my muscles. I lie there, listening to my wife breathe, and wait to fall asleep myself. Something clicks in the back of my wife's throat when she sleeps. I imagine it is the last sound someone might make before they die. I know that my daughter could start up again at any moment. Her distress stays with me like the pain of a burn long after she has drifted off. Falling asleep is like putting my head between the jaws of a lion.

Keep it open, I think to myself, keep it open, but I am no longer talking about a lion and instead thinking of a door that connected me to the outside world when I lay in bed at night as a boy.

I was terrified of the dark. 'You'll never learn,' my stepfather would say, 'if I don't teach you.'

Then the door shuts.

May and I have left the toilet and returned to the library. I sink into a chair with my book of ancient history. I start flicking through the pages, reading summaries of the lives of late Roman emperors, and how they spent their time going mad or patching up ruptured borders, chasing barbarians out of the disintegrating limbs of the empire, quelling mutinies of their own armies. The decline of civilisation, onset of the dark ages, all of that.

I reflect on how daunting it must have been for an emperor to wake up every morning to one problem after another, making decisions that could wipe out cities or nations, just to keep something going for a few decades more. It fascinates me how all the intricate and bloody struggles of countless human beings over several decades can be shoehorned into a couple of paragraphs on a piece of paper. So many people can disappear between those words.

A familiar-looking mother walks past, glances at my daughter and then at me.

'Gosh, she's grown. It goes so *fast*, doesn't it?'

'Yes,' I reply. 'It does.'

'Make the most of it.'

'Okay,' I say, fighting the urge to salute. 'I will.'

I don't say anything else and the woman walks off. My daughter has come to sit in the chair beside me. She has collected a pile of books and makes a show of reading one. We read together for a little while in silence. May lifts one sandalled foot onto the chair cushion and hums softly as she pushes it back and forth in a dreamy way. I note this from the corner of my eye and then turn to look at her more directly. She is pushing something with that foot, and when I look closely I realise that it is shit. It's vital stuff, shit, a sure sign of life, as compelling as any book. I pick her up and put her on the floor.

'Don't move.'

The shit is all over the chair. I glance from this to her legs and see streaks of it along her thighs, a clump hanging like a pendulum on the inside of her shorts. It is all over the floor, too. She's just been to the toilet. Where did this all come from? I feel like I have just woken up, like I'm still groggy, trying to disentangle myself from my own thoughts.

'Don't you *dare* move!'

I take out a wipe and run it across the chair. I succeed in spreading the shit over the cushion, turning it into the kind of economical yet expressive flourish you might see in a Japanese symbol. I back away, feel myself flush with despair, pick up several clumps from the carpet, fold them in a wipe, drop them into my pocket and look towards the service desk, where a young woman runs a stack of books under the scanner.

'Look, Daddy!' My daughter's voice rings through the quiet. 'More poo, there on the carpet. And there!'

I have some on my fingers. Everyone will turn around soon to see me and my poo-stained hands standing in the middle of this mess. My daughter will be happy to point out the sights. She is giggling with delight. I grab her hand and pull her small, light body along.

As we pass the woman at the service desk I loudly declare, 'We don't have any books!'

Several people glance across. I feel like I'm smuggling drugs through customs.

In the toilet, I clean my daughter up the best I can. I am infuriated at her betrayal. 'Why didn't you tell me sooner? Why?'

I throw her pants in a plastic bag, put another bag against her bare arse—it sticks there without a problem and flutters sadly as I put her in the pram. She's finally realised how upset I am and doesn't even attempt to sing. We begin walking home at a brisk pace. She quietly asks for her wrap. She likes to put the corner in her mouth and suck on it for comfort.

'No,' I snarl at her. 'Not your wrap. You're not getting your damn wrap! Don't even *ask* for it again!'

There's shit everywhere: in the pram, on her belly, on the plastic bag flapping up between her legs, tar-like and sticky. I don't want it getting into her mouth. It's not as bad as I think, I tell myself. I'll probably look back on this and laugh. There are other libraries I can go to around the city. Maybe there's a witness protection program for people who leave shit in chairs for other people to sit in.

My daughter begins sobbing.

'Not a sound out of you!' My voice is getting louder. Some people across the road look over at me. This makes me more ashamed and angry at May all at once. I know that I'm being an arsehole, but I know it only from a distance. 'All you have to do is tell me when you need to do a poo, or afterwards. You don't *sit* in it and play with it! Not at the library! Daddy's not happy at all. When we get home, you're getting a bath and going to bed. I don't even want to *talk* to you anymore.'

We walk on in silence. My daughter chokes back her tears. When we get home, I put her under the shower. I wash her without any tenderness and even stick her head under the shower, which makes her finally break into sobs. Then I put her pyjamas on and put her into her bed. Only then do I stop moving and look down at her. My daughter has put her wrap in her mouth. She feeds the corner between her lips and works it with a slight, repetitive motion of her jaw. Her sad blue eyes are turned up at me.

'All you have to do is tell me,' I say softly, the conviction, the rage, draining out of me.

She nods. I stand over her and think suddenly of how small she is—her nose the size of my thumbnail—and how tall I must seem, the fury written on my face, my hands hanging by my sides. My hands are very different from how I remember my stepfather's, but suddenly they feel just as heavy. I walk out of the bedroom and stand in the middle of the living room, staring out the window at the cliffs overlooking the ocean in the distance.

When I return to her bedroom, my daughter doesn't notice at first, or pretends not to. She lies on her side looking up at the ceiling, her small jaw still working away. Then her gaze slides towards me.

I stare down at her. 'Want a hug?'

She nods and I pick her up, hold her body against mine, and I shudder with love and self-loathing. My daughter frees an arm from my embrace and points down at the floor.

'No poo,' she declares with a solemn sweep of her arm. 'No poo anywhere.'

'Yes,' I concede, 'wonderful. You want some lunch?'

My daughter wants rice bubbles and I feed her two bowls, although she knows very well how to do it herself. After that she goes to sleep without a sound. I lie on my bed and doze, only snapping out of it when the door to the apartment opens and shuts.

When I walk into the living room, my wife throws me a smile. My wife and I are always throwing each other smiles and expressions. They are barely caught, as if we are keeping something up in the air doomed to give in to gravity sooner or later.

'How was your morning?'

I tell her that it was okay. I look away. I get my stuff together, kiss her on the cheek and leave the house. I tell her that I'll be back soon, but as I close the front door, I imagine myself leaving her for good.

~

When my older brother and I get together for a drink, he talks sometimes about the past and the way he used to beat me. He doesn't get it. He doesn't know why he did it; he feels like it wasn't him.

Who was it, then?

I tell him that it's fine, that I understand. He still doesn't know where his anger comes from, when he gets drunk, for example, and something happens to make it boil up.

'Do you know what your father did with our money?' my mother asked me one day. 'He spent it on boys, when we were living in London. Prostitutes. That's where your father spent his nights in London and then in Holland.

And that's where he was when you were born. That's why we were so poor.'

I wish this was the most unpleasant thing that I knew of him.

And my stepfather—who immigrated to Australia with us, bringing with him his rich soil of curses—has also become no more than stories and memories, the sort that uncoil inside your head even when you don't want them to. I have an image of him tamping down his pipe, lifting it to his mouth, hidden in the dense mass of his beard, cupping the lighter close with his other hand and making the tight knot of tobacco at the centre flare into life. That sense I have of his heavy calmness and how quickly it could change.

I have never hit my daughter. I never would. But when you have such a past, there is an awareness of the possibilities, a question that stays with you, that aches whenever you stray near.

When my daughter spent the night with me, after my divorce, she slept more soundly. I would stand at the doorway of her room and think of the men who stood at the threshold of mine—who stand there still—and what they have left in me.

No further than this, I warn them. No further. I watch her sleeping, the peacefulness of her expression, and feel better about the world. She sleeps through the nights, although sometimes she still wakes when she is sick or restless. I don't make her go back to sleep but let her sit beside me on the couch while I read a book. She is happy to be there, to eat a sandwich, to watch a cartoon and glance over occasionally with a knowing smile, as if we are both visiting someone else.

10

Con wants to know what I'm writing about. I tell him that I'm writing about him and me, when we were young.

Con has a quality that women find fascinating. It's based around a boyish glint in his eyes, the way it plays against his smile. Our father had that same expression, even when his hair was dead white and years of smoking had pulled his skin into an ashen mask. I have many of my father's features: the same angular cheeks, his nose, even his forehead with its egg-like fragility at the temples. But the likeness goes when I show my teeth. Somehow I have inherited the features and Con has inherited the pose that brings my father to life, the grin that flashes across his face like sunlight on a mirror.

My brother is standing in front of me, with his girlfriend, in the pub. He hooks one arm around her waist, holds a drink loosely in front of him and flashes that smile towards me.

'I hope you haven't portrayed me as some sort of monster,' he says.

A girl with a restless gaze and silky bob of dark hair shifts on her seat beside me. She is one of several women my brother has introduced me to in the year since my divorce. He says that I need the practice, that I need to get back in the game.

'I get the feeling that we're being watched,' the girl murmurs with the straw of her drink angled against her lips.

I try an offhand shrug. 'We are, but who cares?'

Her glance stabs my way. I don't know how to read it. I don't know what to do with my body, where to put it.

My brother suddenly steps close. 'Mate, you need to loosen up.'

He says it loud, with that relaxed grin on his face. He undoes the top button of my shirt, and then the next one.

'We have to bring out the Greek in you.'

I'm here only because of him. A song comes on. My brother steps back and begins dancing. He's in his mid-thirties, his prime. In the last few years, his features have shifted, as if an invisible river is wearing down the angles of his nose and cheeks, though his body is still trim and well-built. Black hair glistens at the opening of his shirt. His broad shoulders roll through the music.

His girlfriend is giggling. She breaks into laughter easily, though there is something brittle in her voice. This is the first time that I've met his girlfriend. I've already noticed that she looks at him a lot more than he does at her. My brother grins as he dances, but it seems to me that something is missing. I see not so much a boy as a man pretending to be a boy. That, too, is my father, or at least how I remember him.

~

The image is an old one. The last time I saw our father, I was thirteen. My mother had succeeded in getting him to pay for my plane ticket back to Holland, the country she had taken us from some three years earlier, the place where he still lived. My father had pleaded to see my brother rather than me. He claimed that it was because my brother was oldest and that this meant a great deal to him as a Greek. It was a matter of tradition.

My mother insisted that he had to see me first. If things went well—and this was a thinly veiled threat—she would return with my older brother next time. It seemed ordinary at the time, but I'm amazed now that this negotiation ever took place. Neither of them should have been considering a reunion—not between themselves, and not between him and us. He was, after all, the main reason that we had abandoned Holland.

My mother and I disembarked at the airport in the middle of winter. My father picked me up while my mother went to stay with my grandmother, whom she had missed intensely, despite their troubled relationship. The plan was that my mother and I would meet again in a few weeks at my aunt's house in the north of Holland.

Apart from one dinner at the house of my grandmother, my mother and I would spend no time together in the intervening period. It was to be the first time in my life that I would have my father to myself.

My father had shrunk and looked skinnier than I remembered. The colour had leached from his olive skin while his hair, black in my memory, now loomed above his forehead like an enormous drift of snow. Something else had changed. As a boy I'd called him Dad—not because I thought of him as my father, but because I thought that was his name. But now I could only call him by his real name, the name that my mother had always used when she spoke of him in a tone that carried both caution and regret.

I called him Andreas.

On the drive to his house I sat in the front seat, staring out at the flat landscape drenched in grey, and it occurred to me that, in the time before my brother and I had gone to Australia, when we used to do things with Andreas, I had never been in the front seat. I was sitting in my brother's place. After a long silence, Andreas glanced at me, then glanced at me again, more searchingly, as if he recognised something, before his eyes fixed back on the road.

'You know,' he said, 'you look just like her.'

My brother and I had been born out of love; that is what my mother always said. But the love went bad and

I wonder now if the love might not have come mainly from my mother.

Andreas drove with his window wound down, despite the cold air. The smile never entirely disappeared from his face—it was always there, at the edges of his mouth, the tug of an irresistible current. A cigarette dangled from his lips. Smoke trailed from the wide, high arches of his nostrils. His eyes cut back to me one more time.

'I have a surprise for you, Michaelis. You'll like it.'

What I didn't like was the Greek use of my name. I especially hated the way that he said it, with its strained lilt in the middle.

When we got to his house, it turned out that the surprise was an old friend of mine, someone I had been in Cub Scouts with as a boy, before I'd left for Australia. The two of us had been kicked out of Cubs after we'd gone out of bounds and climbed into the attic of the building where we were staying during a camp. We'd been caught because I had fallen through the roof. I hadn't seen him again after that.

Max was fourteen, only a year ahead of me, but he seemed much older to me now. I had no idea how he had come to befriend my father. He had the same lank blond hair that I remembered, and a thin, corded neck. He pulled a cigarette from the packet that Andreas offered, lit it and showed me a trick. He drew deep and exhaled into a tissue. Revealing the yellowish-brown nicotine stain on the inside of the tissue, he told me with a cynical grin that this was why you shouldn't smoke. He and my father chuckled like war veterans, glanced at one another and pulled on their cigarettes.

Max did karate and he was eager to demonstrate his training regimen. While Andreas looked on, he jerked his body through a series of moves, and he showed me how to do short, sharp push-ups against a wall. Lots of repetitions, Max told me, that was how you got speed and strength in your punches. He did a hundred of those push-ups every day. His arms were milky, lean pillars of muscle. After this, we all sat around a table and had arm wrestles. He could beat Andreas easily with all of that karate conditioning. So could I.

'You're growing up, Michaelis,' Andreas told me in his oddly pitched tone, still saturated with Greek. 'Turning into a real man, yes, an *animaaale*!'

Memories came to me then of being chased around by him in his pyjamas, him on all fours, my brother and I on our feet, running and dodging and laughing. But he always caught us. I had the impulse to look over my shoulder, like Con might be standing in the hallway behind me now. I smiled at my father and felt a mixture of pride and disappointment. I didn't say how startled I was at his physical smallness, the weakness in his arm, the way I had been able to wrestle it to the table. I wonder now if he had been letting me win. He could be very convincing in his deceptions.

Still breathing hard from his karate moves, Max lit up another cigarette and turned to Andreas. 'You should show Mike your videos.'

Andreas raised his eyebrows. 'I think he's a bit young for that sort of thing, aren't you, Michaelis?'

'I'm not too young at all,' I said quickly.

'Come on,' Max urged. 'He can look away if he doesn't like it.'

'What would your mother think?' Andreas stared at me, but flicked his eyes over my shoulder at Max, his mouth hooked at one end as if they were sharing a private joke. His voice was crooning and persuasive when he lowered it.

I told him that I didn't care what my mother thought. She was far away, and I was a man now.

'Just remember, Michaelis, that a *man* doesn't have to tell his mother everything,' he said as he put on the video.

He didn't need to convince me of that. I had long since started keeping secrets from my mother. I sat on the couch beside Max. There was a flicker of static on the screen, a rush of indistinct noise before the image kicked in. It was a foreign movie, German. We watched a woman in a nurse's uniform force her hand inside another woman's vagina.

'Look at that.' Max leaned into his crossed arms and tensed his fists so that veins rose into the pale skin. 'Yeah, give it to her. Give it to her.'

'Don't get ash on my couch,' Andreas said, ruffling his hair.

He put an ashtray beside Max and kept on tidying the house, making sure that it was as clean and carefully ordered as the moment I had walked in. The ceiling was low and pale. All of the walls were white. A couple of generic photography prints were hung on the walls in simple glass frames: a waterfall, a lighthouse. The neatness of the place was disrupted only by a plant that had outgrown its pot. Its tendrils, thick as femoral arteries, shot along the window frame and up to the ceiling; its fleshy leaves dangled along the architraves. Glancing at it from where I sat on the couch, I imagined that the plant would keep growing forever, that it would find its way into every room of the house.

'You have the best fucking dad,' Max said suddenly.

I watched him briefly, swallowing and drawing at the cigarette between his wet lips, exhaling smoke through his nose exactly the way my father did. My eyes pulled back towards the television, where a man had joined the two women. I had a hard-on. I was grinning; the muscles of my cheeks strained at my jaw. My heart shuddered against the bottom of my throat. But I kept on watching. Most of all, I felt a shameful relief that my brother couldn't see me.

Usually the things that I kept hidden from my mother were secrets that I shared with Con. He did the bulk of the lying. It was my job to stay quiet. When we still lived in Holland, he took me once to a place shut off from the world by a tall barbed-wire fence. Signs on the fence said 'Keep Out' and 'Danger'. Con had found a slit cut into the wire and he held it open as he stared back at me. He was eleven and I was eight.

'You're too young for this,' he said. 'You'll only get us into trouble. You should wait here.'

I told him that I wasn't too young, that I could look after myself.

'Okay,' he said. 'But do exactly what I tell you.'

I did not want to go through the fence at all, but I was determined to follow him. It was the only way that I could feel close to him. We passed a shooting range, and long chains that looked like they were used to tie up dogs. Paths ran between oaks and pines and past concrete structures with locked metal doors. We came to a place where a huge tree spread its branches beside a narrow road.

Nearby I could see a building punctured by lights, and people moving around inside. I wanted to stay out of sight and take no chances. The tree facing us had released a sea of tiny nuts. My brother strolled forward, squatted among the nuts in plain view and began eating them. He turned and looked at where I was cowering in the bushes.

He flashed me his grin. 'They taste good, Michaelis.'

There was never a hint of fear in him at these moments. As I started walking, a man in an army uniform came riding past on a bike. When he saw us, everything changed. The world snapped into sharp lines of tension and adrenalin. The man grunted, stumbled off his bike and ran towards us with a tight, focused expression. It was the kind of look that I'd seen on my stepfather's face a hundred times and I knew what it meant. My brother was off. He yelled at me to run too, and I did, but the distance between us grew with each panting step, and my brother was out of reach, silent and fluid-limbed, not even looking back. I ran as fast as I could. My ankle jarred against a hole in the ground. I stumbled, then kept running. The man behind me was surprisingly quick on his feet. When I felt his breath right on my neck, I turned around.

'Stay away from me!' I warned in a shrill voice.

He seized me by the back of my shirt, lifted me as if I weighed nothing and carried me towards the building with the lights on inside.

By the time my brother came home, hours later, darkness pressed against the windows of our house. I sat at the dinner table with my mother and stepfather.

Dirk shoved back his chair and glared at my brother. 'Where have you been? Don't you know it's dinnertime? What have you been up to?'

Dirk had a way of standing right over us when he asked questions, his shoulders bunched around his neck. My brother glanced across at me, sitting there beside our mother. He had straight, dark hair and my father's brilliant hazel eyes like polished wood. They were eyes that turned hard in anger, though now they were full of curiosity. With the air of someone repeating a well-worn story, he said that he'd lost me while we were out playing.

My stepfather turned and I felt his gaze on me like a dead weight. We were eating sandwiches for dinner. I chewed on my sandwich and shrugged.

Later, as we lay on the separate levels of our bunk bed, I whispered to my brother about how I'd been made to sit in a room with fluorescent lights, a bunch of men in uniforms around me. They had looked at me until I had started crying. Then they had given me a glass of orange juice and a biscuit and walked me to the front gate and told me never to come back.

'I waited at the fence for hours,' my brother said softly.

I thought that he'd pile abuse on me then for not having run quick enough, but he remained silent. It occurred to me suddenly that he was ashamed of having abandoned me. I liked that thought. I had done the right thing, though, by staying silent. These were the important things: to not ask, to not tell.

Let him do the lying.

Despite the separateness of our lives, my brother and I shared a room for most of our childhoods. On the whole, I would have been terrified of sleeping alone, but it was still an uneasy coexistence. I grew up knowing the story of how, in the months after I was born, he had tried to bury me. He would scour the room for objects that he could pile into my cot: toys, clothes, footwear.

Later, he usually ignored me, but there were moments when he didn't. My mother told him off once for arranging a packet's worth of thumbtacks in my bed. With an attention to detail that he rarely displayed elsewhere, he had laid the tacks out carefully with the points facing up and draped the bedsheet over them. My mother discovered them when she put me to bed. She told him that it was his responsibility to look after me, that we only had each other.

My brother's violence often came unexpectedly. It never stayed on the surface long. When he fought other people, he beat them quickly and efficiently, no matter how much bigger or stronger they were, and while they were still nursing bloody noses he'd be off doing something else, smiling like the whole thing had never happened.

In the same way, not long after his attacks on me, he would come strolling back into view, preoccupied with something else, a pleasant grin on his face when he glanced in my direction. His whole expression would dazzle me, invite me to forget, to share the joke, to get into the present where he lived his life, and I would find it impossible to maintain my fury. But during the time I spent alone with my father, far away from my brother, I started seeing that smile differently.

~

Despite my father's efforts, my stay with him did not turn out well. A week earlier than planned, he drove me to my aunt's house to reunite me with my mother. We hardly spoke on that trip. He stopped along the way for a cake. It was a piece of art: a large, circular structure of pastry brimming with dark, pitted cherries and dusted with icing sugar. When we arrived, he smiled, held the cake aloft in one hand, and stepped over the threshold into my aunt's house. He was welcome there. My aunt couldn't stop gushing over the cake and nearly everyone was full of admiration. It was as if they were welcoming a long-lost friend.

The only one in the house that didn't seem impressed with his arrival was my mother. I sensed that she was having some kind of ongoing argument with my aunt—a fat, jolly woman ten years older who had always played something of the role of a mother to her. My aunt was boisterous and could shove a joking comment into any conversation. It was hard not to be charmed by her even when she was thrusting an opinion down your throat.

One of the things I overheard her saying was, 'Come on now, regardless of what did or didn't happen, a boy deserves to *know* his father.'

When my father and I had stopped for the cake, we had gone into a mall and window-shopped for a while, and had an argument that simmered for hours afterwards. I had wanted him to buy me a samurai sword. The blade was wavy hammered steel, and it had a glossy black scabbard inlaid with fake gold flowers and images of tigers and dragons. I'd developed a fascination for swords ever since I'd watched *Conan the Barbarian* as a six-year-old. I used to draw them obsessively. I'd imagine using them on my stepfather in all sorts of elaborate scenarios. Andreas said no to the sword because he was becoming used to my asking for things and growing tired of it. And I was upset because I was becoming used to getting what I wanted from him.

And while this dynamic disturbed me, I couldn't stop. I didn't know why I was asking him for things all the time. I was thirteen, had begun working after school back at home, and knew what it was like to earn my own possessions. But I had discovered a sort of power over Andreas. He was offering me things with a subdued, domestic urgency, fussing over me in a way that leant him an air of fallibility. Or apology. Or guilt. He was constantly checking to see if I had what I wanted, doing it in a way that both irritated me and brought out my predatory instinct. He had ignored me for most of my life; I wanted to take him for all he was worth.

And then I told him that I wanted to leave his house a week early because I missed my mother and wanted to spend some time with my cousins. Andreas was hurt, though I think he was also relieved because no matter what he bought me I didn't seem to be satisfied or happy. I didn't tell him the real reason that I wanted to leave. I think he probably knew.

At one point towards the end of my stay with him,

he gave me money to buy a record. I bought Queen's *Greatest Hits* and put it on at full blast in his house. He listened tolerantly the whole way through. He watched me with a kind of curiosity bordering on affection as I played air guitar to 'Seven Seas of Rhye'. Max was there, doing his endless push-ups against the wall.

When the song finished, Andreas smiled and told me suddenly that he still cared about my mother. He said that she was a lovely person, but just unstable, prone to imagining things that weren't there. Or, he added with a confident glance towards Max, things that had never happened.

It was then that I made up my mind about him.

On the last day of the trip to Holland, Andreas reappeared with his car and drove my mother and I back to the airport. Everyone except my mother said that it was a lovely and generous gesture, because he lived on the other side of the country and had driven three hours to get to us. My mother reluctantly accepted my father's help and thanked him in a stilted sort of way. By then, I think my mother regretted giving in to her feelings of longing and coming back to Holland, and involving my father with it all.

It was strange being in the back of my father's car, watching the two of them in front, as if I had tumbled into some alternate future where they were still together. Andreas began discussing with a feverish kind of enthusiasm the possibility of seeing my brother the next time Mum came to Holland. He wanted to know everything about him: what he was doing, what his ambitions were, whether he had a girlfriend yet.

Andreas had always been fascinated by my brother's love-life. The distance to the airport shrank in the silence of the early morning outside. I imagined my brother sitting in the front seat instead of my mother. I was quiet, brooding on the strange things that had happened during my time with my father. My mother must have thought that I was quiet for an entirely different reason.

All of a sudden, she said, 'Mike has all these wonderful qualities that you've just never seen. How could you not see them?'

'Look,' Andreas said, 'I guess I just never really noticed them because he's so different to me.'

'Different, how?'

'You know, sensitive, fragile. A bit like...'

'Me?'

'Maybe, maybe,' he said. He then added, with his peculiar foreign manner of phrase, that my brother was easier to love.

'Why?' my mother asked.

'He's more in my—how do I put it?—*image*.'

The unabashed way in which he said this while I sat in the car with him struck me with a kind of awe. I don't remember how this conversation ended. It was getting lighter and trees shot up from the flat landscape like spearheads into the smoky sky.

Andreas hugged me at the airport and I kissed the cheek he offered. The well-kept surface, with its hint of stubble and a sophisticated aftershave whiff, still evoked in me an instinctive admiration, and a distilled sort of happiness, and I remembered how seeing my father when I was a kid for our brief times together had meant the headlong rush into a most wonderful and seductive feeling of potential. But that was nostalgia, and my real feelings meant now that I didn't look back at him as we walked away.

I would never see him again, in the flesh. My mother and I got on the plane and sat together in silence. Relief was all that I could feel. The plane taxied along the runway. Grey pressed on the flat landscape, making it vague, and rain sliced across the narrow window beside me. The plane turned and paused. Then it jolted forward and raced along the tarmac with a shudder. Ash-coloured cloud filled the window, then tore away to reveal a dazzling, clear sky, a sun as bright and fierce as any summer's day in Australia. It was surprising to see that sky, to remember that it existed, far from the weight of winter and the detail of the ground.

~

Now I am studying my face in a mirror and thinking of him as I direct a frothy stream of piss into the urinal beneath it. I am trying to be objective, weighing my seductive potential. Chest hair shows at the unbuttoned juncture of my shirt. I try to give myself a charming smile. I do what my brother has told me: I draw on my inner Greek. I have no idea what that means. I don't know a word of Greek. And I don't know the place that my father came from. Con sometimes pretends to know, but his memories are the memories of a child.

Cyprus, my mother used to tell me, was the island upon which Aphrodite, the goddess of love, first set foot. It's a romantic story until you learn that Aphrodite was born from the castrated genitals of her father.

I make my way back into the crowded bar and return to the place where my brother is holding court. He's just been on a diving trip to Fiji and talk has turned to sharks. I try to mirror his ease, and slide my way next to the girl.

'I hate swimming in the ocean,' she says, 'because I always think of sharks.'

'I'd bet you'd feel fine if you went with me,' I tell her when the bustle of the pub separates us momentarily from the others.

Her eyes dart around the room. I lean towards her. She uses my hands to gently leverage me away.

'Don't,' she says.

I slump back on my chair, half relieved, and the noise of the pub presses around me. She gives a slight shrug, gets to her feet and goes off with my brother's girlfriend to the toilet. With his girlfriend gone, my brother's demeanour changes. His gaze moves across the women in the pub with a hungry intensity before it comes to rest on me. He looks at me for a moment as if he doesn't recognise me, then his gaze clears.

'How's it going, Mike?'

'I'm lonely.'

'Ah, I know the feeling.' He exudes a sudden melancholic air. 'Me too. Yeah. God. I'm still in love with Monika. Do you remember how good we were together? I'm going to Sweden on my next holiday, and I'll see if I can give her one last shot.'

'Aren't you in love with your actual girlfriend?'

His lips press inwards and his face softens into that desolate place. 'Almost, but no. It's just not *there*.'

I want to ask him all sorts of questions but his girlfriend returns and that sad, open expression on his face vanishes. A new song comes on. My brother undoes another button on his own shirt, and begins dancing again, the moves sexier, more absurd than before. I can't stop looking at his face, the deceptive ease in the eyes, in the motion of his body. He doesn't look lonely, not one bit. I know, though, that Monika has left him for good. And he wasn't sure about her until she did.

He invites me to join him now with a dazzling, comradely nod. The girl that I tried to kiss is leaning over her cranberry and vodka and staring at my brother. His girlfriend is also watching his display. She shakes her head with loving good humour, then gets up and joins him. He dances like he has known his girlfriend all of his life, like he will never leave her.

'Come on, Mike,' my brother says.

I am sick from too much alcohol and feel as if someone has poured glue into my heart. I want no part of this. I know that I can't do it in the way that my brother does. I only look awkward when I try.

I start dancing.

~

It was the height of summer when I returned to Australia. My brother didn't ask much about Andreas. He had always seemed slightly bored by our father and his only disappointment appeared to be that he'd missed out on seeing his childhood friends.

'Andreas says nothing happened,' I told him a few weeks after my return.

We were sitting on the couch. My brother was watching the cricket. He could sit there in front of the television for hours when the cricket was on, his face as unmoving as the faces on the screen.

'What do you mean?' he asked.

'Between you and him. He says Mum made it all up, that she's unstable.'

Con laughed. I mentioned seeing my friend Max with Andreas quite a bit, although I didn't say what we'd watched together.

'Yeah,' my brother said. 'Some of the guys on my soccer team used to hang at his house, all the time, even when I wasn't around.'

He turned to me and gave me a brief smile. He had a way of smiling without showing his teeth that had nothing to do with putting on charm. Something bleak would come into his face.

By this stage, our father had phoned up a couple of times. He had already begun talking of seeing my brother in the coming year, of making the arrangements. The next time he phoned, my brother asked to speak to him.

'Andreas.' Con spoke softly into the phone. He listened for a moment, then said, 'I hate your fucking guts. You're a sick coward. Don't call here again.'

He put down the phone and went into his room. He came out with his spearfishing gear.

'It's blowing a westerly,' he told me. 'Bet the water's dead flat.'

He took me out spearfishing for the first time during that summer. We plunged off the rocks together and started paddling out towards the tankers on the horizon. We paddled for twenty minutes, way past the shark nets. I was terrified of sharks. I couldn't see the bottom, only islands of shadow and strange turns of light, and fish, longer than my arms, sliding past as if I didn't exist.

Every now and again, my brother kicked down and left me drifting above him in a cloud of bubbles. I didn't know how to follow him down. Alone, at the surface, I shivered and choked at each watery breath in my snorkel until I saw him rising towards me. Often when he did, the carcass of a fish hung from his spear. He nearly always managed to shoot fish in the eye. When he was nearby, I lifted my head and stared back longingly at the thin ribbon of the shoreline, but the thought of paddling back alone filled me with a sickening fear.

By the time we returned to shore, I could not feel my hands or feet and my teeth chattered so fiercely that I thought they would shatter. I asked him whether he ever got scared out there by himself.

'No,' he told me.

'What do you think of when you're out there?'

He showed his teeth. 'Nothing. The fish.'

My brother was sixteen years old by then, well proportioned and broad-shouldered. My own limbs were longer and thinner and had always felt strange to me. His short, dark hair was tousled and rough with salt water. He crouched with one knee on the rocks and opened the belly of each of his fish with a practised motion. He tossed fistfuls of guts to the seagulls that wheeled and descended around us.

While he stared back over the blue drape of the ocean, he remarked that he was impressed with how I had stayed out with him for nearly two hours. He had come prepared, in a thick rubber wetsuit, while I wore only my swimmers. I had never heard him say that before, that he was *impressed* with me.

I had recently begun wearing my brother's old clothes. He never handed them down to me—he sold them. He would throw his old things away if he didn't get the price he wanted. I often bought the clothes from him, but they never sat well on me. I was too skinny and his clothes were already worn by the time they got to me; I looked like a scarecrow. So I focused on the way I had seen my brother wear them, the ease with which he moved inside his skin.

My brother's friends used to call me by his name. They added *junior* at the end, as if I were his son. But apart from the history we shared, I was more aware of our difference. My brother had a broad Australian accent and blended into school in every way. My own accent still carried the thick, stumbling textures of Holland. I was much taller than the people around me, and solitary.

My brother could pick up any sort of sporting implement and act like he had been using it for years, and he had an easy contempt for those who didn't have that natural ability.

'Have you actually seen yourself try to surf?' he said to me when he was eighteen, without looking at me. 'It's the funniest thing I've ever seen.'

I flew into a rage. I stood in front of him and screamed at him. I described in great detail how he had always put me down, how he had oppressed me, made my life hell, despite the fact that I had only ever admired him. He turned white, as if all of this was news to him, and for once he did not lash back. After that, he never hit me again, and he'd occasionally find ways of praising me. He'd tell me that I was better with words than he was, that I was the clever one.

All of this runs through my mind as we walk home together from the pub. He's different when we are alone together, out in the open air, more like the boy I remember following when we were young. The boy that I admired without question. I have the urge to make a connection with him. We live in different cities. Our lives are more separate than ever. I decide to tell him something that I've never told anyone. I tell him that I watched porn at our father's house, twenty years ago.

His footsteps don't even falter. His expression remains fixed. 'Really? Why didn't you tell me earlier?'

'Dunno.' I can feel myself blushing all of a sudden. 'It felt like a betrayal, I guess. I was ashamed. No idea why I did it, either. I just wanted him to *like* me, to include me in things.'

Con laughs softly. 'That's why I used to get so angry at you. You had no idea what that would have meant.'

We walk on in silence.

'Good old Andreas,' my brother says after a moment. 'I wonder what he looks like now.'

'Probably smaller than you'd think.'

'Yeah.'

'Reckon you'll ever see him again?'

'Don't know. It'd be funny, wouldn't it?'

He makes a playful kick at a bottle lying on the footpath and pushes his hands into the pockets of his jeans. I haven't seen him play soccer in a long time, though he has a habit of kicking at things—pieces of rubbish, plants, the occasional cat. He does it without seeming to notice.

'Yeah, funny all right,' I say.

I walk beside him and think of how strange it is to have such a father in our lives, for the two of us to be bound together and separated in that way.

When our father surfaces in our conversation we call him 'Dad' once or twice for comic effect, but we always fall back into Andreas, because it is easier to resort to the ironic distance of his name. We sometimes argue about who looks more like him, and it's me, of course, but I can't put on his voice the way my brother does. And my father's smile, with its easy confidence, its charm, that too passed down only to my brother.

I stare across at Con, his face set, that brilliant glint in his dark eyes. I tell him that we have never talked about what happened between him and Andreas, that I'd like to. The thought terrifies me, but a part of me needs to know just more than the hazy detail. I know that he won't tell Mum anything else. He says that he wants her to sleep at night. He shows his teeth and then stares off down the road.

'We'll talk about it,' he says. 'We'll have a beer and talk about it some day.'

11

I've never been good at playing the host, and now my mother has come to stay for an indefinite period. Our first run-in is over a cup of tea. Before the fight, we go to a cafe. I walk ahead with my girlfriend, Emily, and my mother hobbles behind on a crutch, my daughter clinging to her free hand. I buy the coffees and we don't talk much as we sit around the table with its view to the ocean, although my mother looks at me sadly sometimes.

Emily and I hug as we walk home. An icy wind lifts from the sea and cuts through our clothes. I glance at my mother and see her struggling in our wake with a world-weary expression, as if she's a refugee from some war carrying all that's left of her belongings on her back. I don't slow down.

When we get home, Emily goes out to do some shopping. I want to lie on the couch in the living room, out of the way, free to roam in my thoughts for a while. My daughter wants to play chess.

'Set up the board,' I tell her, stifling a yawn.

The house doesn't feel like mine yet. Emily and I have only been here five weeks—we've barely finished unpacking the boxes, and now my mother is here. Still yawning, I get up and wander into the kitchen. If I'm going to get through the day, I need something more to wake me up. I put the kettle on, take the teapot on my kitchen bench, and drop in some Earl Grey. My mother loves a cup of tea. You always have to pour your guests the first cup of coffee and the last cup of tea—that's what she used to tell me, just like her mother before her. I repeat the words now in Dutch, to myself.

I watch her through the window, in the courtyard hunched over the book, broken ankle slung before her. I fill the pot with boiling water and glance at her one last time, sitting there all alone. Then I take my tea into the living room.

My mother is in mourning because she has just separated from the man in her life. While I spent a few holidays around him, much of what I know about Brian comes from the stories my mother told me.

He is fourteen years older than her. They met because they walked every evening along the same beach on the Gold Coast. I was there when they first spoke. He said hello, commented on the weather and walked on. I noticed a gold stud in one ear, a finely trimmed grey beard, and a watery looseness in his gaze.

'What do you think of him?' my mother asked as she glanced at him striding off in his white linen pants rolled up to the shins.

I told my mother that I wasn't sure.

Brian had a PhD in theology, but he didn't believe in God anymore. He suffered from a degenerative lung disease and couldn't kiss with his tongue because he ran out of breath. His lips were thin and dry and tasted like the medication he took, so it was something of a relief anyway. He was also impotent. He made up for this, my mother said, with a passionate personality.

Things did not take long to go sour between them. As their relationship began its long, slow disintegration, and my mother began to voice her doubts, he would come into her room at night, stand over her bed, and yell at her in his hoarse, wounded voice. He called her a bastard, a tyrant and a traitor.

'You promised to look after me until I died,' he'd shout. 'And now you've made me waste some of the best years of my life!'

He'd shout at her until dawn peeled away night. Then he'd go to bed to rest his exhausted lungs. He was approaching seventy, having retired at sixty-two, and he possessed the freedom of the days. Looking at his leather-bound events diary and appraising the hours available to him with a pen held to his dry lips, he often said that he wished he were dead. My mother told me sometimes that she felt as if she too were approaching seventy. Not a good seventy. She began talking more and more about leaving him to his misery, getting on with her own life, but one thing or another always held her back.

'Maybe,' my mother would say, 'he'll just die one day soon. You know? The universe always comes up with a solution.'

My daughter is sitting cross-legged on the table, her chin on one hand. When I play chess with her, I have to find ways of convincing her that she's winning, and also that I am doing my best to prevent this. May is now six and I have no idea where her passion for the game has come from. Checkmate, I tell her. She looks from the board to me, and back again, and realises that she's beaten me. Disappointment flashes across her face. We've played two games and she wants to play a third.

'No,' I tell her. 'It's time to take your Nan to the shops.'

My mother needs new furniture. She gets over relationship breakdowns by giving away as much as she can. I still have a lovely pair of nineteenth-century bronze candle-holders from a ship that she handed over to me at the end of her last relationship. They're designed with hinges so that the candles always stay level. The ship might be going down, but at least you'll be able to see the looks on people's faces, the water coming in. As for the current batch of furniture, Brian said that he wanted it, but now he's changed his mind and it is all sitting unclaimed in a shed in Myrtleford, the Victorian country town they moved to a few years after he retired.

'This is Brian,' my mother tells me. 'This is exactly Brian.'

Myrtleford is set among hills that were for a long time draped in lush green tobacco plantations. Myrtleford also used to be home to the Big Cigarette, a smoke stack painted to resemble a monstrous cigarette, defiantly thrust upwards from a tobacco-drying factory.

Brian was never able to make many friends in this town. He said that it was the small-mindedness of country people, that it made them so aloof, difficult to communicate with, and resistant to ideas broader than their own. My mother told me that it was because he talked at people in this relentless way. He cornered them and didn't listen to a word they said, lifting and raising one finger at them like he was conducting an invisible orchestra. After that, they would cross the street to avoid him.

Things must have changed somewhere along the line, or perhaps they didn't, but after the break-up, he warned my mother never to come back. It was his town now.

The door to the living room opens. My mother hobbles in and puts down her Holocaust book.

'Okay, I'm ready to go out and do some shopping! It feels like the dawn of a new era, don't you think?'

I nod, walk past her into the hallway, and stop beside the discoloured statue of an elephant, sitting on a cupboard near the front door. My mother gave me that elephant for my birthday, years ago. It's cast in a single piece of bronze, and imported from India. When she gave it to me, it reeked of exotic spices deep in its hollow legs. My mother told me that it was over a hundred years old, that families in India were selling off these things so that they could buy washing machines and other electrical appliances. She thought it was a perfect gift for me, because she'd really wanted it for herself. She said that it could be our family heirloom. Right now, the trunk of the elephant is pointing away from the door. It always needs to be pointing at the door for good fortune; otherwise it's bad luck.

My mother speaks suddenly at my back. 'Did you have a cup of tea?'

I turn and follow her gaze to the teapot, still there beside the cup, on the coffee table. My mother is waiting for an answer. I wonder if I should tell a lie, but the pot is probably still warm to the touch.

With one hand I straighten the elephant. 'Yes. I did have a cup of tea.'

She stares at me. 'Why didn't you ask me if I wanted one?'

Now I do decide to lie. 'I didn't think of it. I just felt like a cup of tea, so I made one.'

My mother looks from me to her plastered foot and back again.

'Well,' she says at last, 'you could have asked me, you know. I wouldn't do that to you. That's not hospitality.'

Hospitality comes from the Latin *hospitalitas*. Buried in this ancient word like a hibernating bear is the root of another word—hostility.

When she first met Brian on that beach on the Gold Coast, my mother was forty-six and newly single after her third divorce. People never believed her when she told them her age. 'Oh, really?' they'd say. 'And these are your *sons*?' She did yoga twice a week, could stand on her head, was paying off her house, and relied on no one for the first time in her life. She was determined to keep it that way.

Brian moved in two years later.

'I knew that it was a mistake,' she told me later. 'I had such a terrible feeling in my stomach when he said that he wanted to move in. Dreadful.'

'Then why did you agree to it?'

'I don't know.' She hesitated. 'Well I *do* know, but it sounds silly. He was crowding me out. He was over at my place all the time anyway. I felt like I couldn't breathe. I thought that if I let him move in with me, I'd get more time to *myself*.'

After he moved in, Brian insisted on having his own room to sleep in. He told her that he'd be damned if he had to share his bed with a woman every night. At first he slept in the second bedroom of her house. When I stayed, I'd lie in the guest bed and hear the breath from his degenerating lungs carry across the floorboards, his cough breaking through like the wounded bark of a neighbourhood dog hemmed in by suburbs, but he rarely seemed to wake himself up.

Sometimes he would get up early in the morning, groan and sigh and hack his lungs clear, and sit in his pyjamas out on the verandah staring at people heading off to work. When kids walked past on their way to school, he would wave at them and shout with vicious enthusiasm, 'Give those teachers *hell*!'

At other times, Brian liked to reminisce about the days when he himself had shaped the minds of young men as a high-school principal. He had left this position when women started teaching in the school, and he became the assistant director of a religious organisation instead. After this job, he retired and moved into my mother's house.

Living in the second bedroom of my mother's house did not please Brian. He offered my mother seventy thousand dollars to convert her garage into a granny flat so that he could live there with the comfort of his things around him. My mother said that she didn't want to owe another man anything again, but he described this money as a gift. Despite her doubts, she relented.

Brian enjoyed working in the garden, though he didn't like living in the converted garage after all—he thought it would work better as his study—and he moved back into the second bedroom. The rooms and corridors of my mother's house became like the arteries of a heart-attack victim, all clogged up. Even the breeze had to bend in half to get through. Every day Brian wandered around the house in a depression that gave way to sudden bouts of rage. 'What is my life *for*?' he would ask.

My mother says it was apparently not for cleaning or cooking. She worked as a nurse and would come home from a ten-hour shift to a messy house and then she would clean and cook for him—he would eat dolefully without noticing the food—and afterwards they would sit on the couch together, crowded in by his possessions, and watch television.

The television kept things quiet. If my mother did her own thing, if she read a book or started painting or talked on the phone for more than five minutes, Brian would pace up and down the house, breathing through his nose in short, agitated bursts.

'That's just great,' he would say at last. 'I guess I'll just amuse *myself* then.'

When I came to visit them, which I did less and less as their relationship developed, Brian would tell me what a remarkable woman my mother was. In his breathy and yet booming voice, with that expository finger bobbing between us, he would describe her strength, her moral courage in the face of all the adversity in her life, and her remarkable beauty and generosity. He would describe these things as if I'd never encountered my mother before, as if he were trying to convince me that, one day, the two of us should meet.

But he would fall into a savage depression if I or anyone else stayed longer than a couple of days. He would lock himself in his room or, in the days when he still lived in his own place, disappear completely. When I or my brothers had gone, he would return and tell my mother that she was far too close to her sons, that it wasn't natural, that a husband should always come before the children.

'But Brian,' she'd tell him, 'we're not married.'

'Oh, we might as well be,' he'd answer morosely. 'We might as damned well be.'

It's two weeks now since the break-up. As we sit together over breakfast, my mother's gaze swivels from Emily to me. There are tired lines in her face, and I wonder if she has slept at all. Her eyes are rimmed in red and have a brittle, glassy appearance, but she's trying for a cheerful smile.

'You two sounded like you were having fun last night, in the bedroom,' she says.

Emily looks across at me. I pretend not to notice.

'Yes,' my mother goes on, stirring her cereal, making a whirlpool, 'it sounded like you were having a great time together. At least someone in this house is. It's been a long time since I've been able to make that claim.'

Emily gets up at that and goes off into the kitchen, where she starts cleaning up, clattering the pans and dishes together more loudly than usual.

'Oh, she's such a good girl, isn't she?' my mother says.

I make myself smile at my mother and follow my girlfriend into the kitchen.

Three years after Brian moved into her house and made it his own, my mother decided that the only way to get rid of him was to sell her house and move to another state. It was as if she was dealing with a catastrophic termite infestation. She sold her house near the coast at a bargain price to one of Brian's friends and moved inland, but Brian decided upon the state and the town, which he had passed through as a young man, and he even chose the house that they would live in together.

'Together?'

I ask my mother how this had happened, when she had only sold the house, which she had loved, and moved in order to leave him. She says that it is a difficult thing to explain. She says that love is mysterious.

I ask her if she was ever in love with Brian.

'I was only ever in love with one man,' she tells me without hesitation, 'and that was your father.'

Working as a nurse in a small country town in Victoria was not a happy change for my mother. The pay was worse and there were no ward assistants, so she had to do her own lifting.

My mother has always been prepared to do her own lifting. When I was a kid, she could rearrange the furniture in a living room in the space of a couple of hours. I'd come home from school to find a different house to the one that I'd left. I used to wonder at that superhuman strength of hers, her energy when it came to shifting anything—the heaviest objects in her house, herself, her family.

Late one night, at the hospital, while attempting to move an obese eighty-year-old from a bed to a chair, my mother crushed part of her spine. It gave way, like old rotten wood supporting a bridge. Childbirth, she says, was nothing compared to the pain she experienced then. And so, at fifty-four, she was finished as a nurse and after three years of punishing legal battles, endless medication, and operations that fused her lower spine but did not cure her terrible pain, she received two hundred thousand dollars to last her for the rest of her life.

During that time, with both of them at home, things deteriorated more rapidly. Brian felt betrayed. He'd been expecting more than two hundred thousand. And although the hospital paid a cleaner to take care of the house and my mother still did all of the cooking, he complained that he had become nothing but a chauffeur, waiting to drive my mother around, hemmed in by her physical limitations.

'Where are your beloved sons now?' he would ask her. 'Why aren't they here now? If they are such good sons, if they really love you, then why aren't they *here* taking care of you?'

I would get these accounts from my mother. I was never sure how she answered or which words were his and which were hers. My relationship with my mother was held together by holiday visits and phone calls since she'd left Newcastle, fifteen years earlier. She'd lived in the Northern Territory, Queensland and Victoria, but she sounded the same when she called me from every place, at least until she started taking the medication for her back. My mother told me that she had trouble thinking and remembering things clearly because of the medication. But whenever she related the things that Brian said about me, I would shift uncomfortably.

Late into the night, I hear her moving around the house. Creaking up and down the stairs, groaning and sighing as she moves between her bedroom and the bathroom, the kitchen and my computer, which she uses to communicate with her sister overseas and my older brother in Sydney.

I am standing under the shower, letting the water prickle on the skin of my face, when the door to the bathroom opens. My mother comes hobbling in and sits down on the toilet. I turn away from her.

'Nothing I haven't seen before,' my mother says.

She does a piss, wipes herself and stands up to peer through the clear glass at me.

'Thanks,' she says, 'for letting me share the bathroom with you, anyway.'

Three weeks have passed since the break-up. Brian phones my mother most days to make sure that it is still over. After breakfast, as we are about to head out to look at places for her to live, he calls her and she retreats with the phone into my daughter's bedroom. I can hear her sobbing. May is sitting at the coffee table, drawing a picture of dinosaurs and an exploding volcano. She is pretending to be entirely focused on the task at hand, but every now and again she glances towards the bedroom.

'Oh, Brian,' my mother keeps saying from the other side of the door. 'Oh, Brian.'

The call ends and she comes out into the living room and stares at all of us.

'He's so abusive,' she says. 'I can't stand it. He kept calling me a fucking bastard, and this and that. Then he told me that he still loves me and wants me back. He says that we're soul mates.'

My mother collapses on the couch and begins crying, big, heart-rending sobs that shake through her whole body.

'I don't know what to do about it all,' she says. 'Really, I don't. I've been through too much in my life. I just can't handle it anymore. I can't.'

May quietly gets up, walks across to her and begins

patting her on the shoulder, like she does with her dolls.

'There, there,' she murmurs. 'It's all right, Nani.'

'He loves me and he wants more money,' my mother goes on, hugging May for a moment. 'He always wants more money.'

'Well,' I say, 'at least you know that about him. Haven't you already given him eighty thousand dollars?'

My mother shrugs. 'He spends it. Now he needs a different car. It's the third car in eighteen months. He buys cars and sells them again for half the price. He makes all these stupid investments. I'm not giving him any more. It's my payout money and I need it to survive and he'll just piss it away.'

'That sounds reasonable.'

'Do you think so?' She looks up at me.

'Of course. You've more than paid him what you weren't even supposed to owe him in the first place.'

'Okay then,' she says. 'If you think so.'

'Don't let him pressure you,' I tell her, falling into my role. 'Don't let him make you feel guilty. You've had enough of men bullying you into what they want you to do.'

She nods and hobbles off to my daughter's room again. I hear the phone ring, and her voice, softer than before.

'I've done it,' she tells me later as we sit down to dinner.

'Done what?'

'Given him the money.' My mother shrugs and doesn't look at me. 'It's only money, Michael. Sometimes you have to be able to see past that.'

I stare at her a moment and then focus on the pizza sitting on the table between us. I begin cutting it into rough slices.

'Well, he got what he wanted from you then.'

'I did it for myself,' she tells me, 'for my own peace of mind. Not for him.' She leans across the table, puts a hand on my arm and stares up into my face with a weary, tolerant smile. 'You know, it's okay to give advice, Michael, but you shouldn't be that way when people don't do exactly what *you* want them to do. That's not being supportive.'

'Okay,' I say, and we start eating.

'I hope you'll have your mother back here again for pizzas every now and again,' she says, swallowing a mouthful of wine, 'after she leaves.'

'Of course.'

My mother wants to live close by. We'll be living in the same city for the first time in fifteen years. She says that we'll be like a proper family again. Every boy needs to have his mother close. On the other hand, she's also been saying that she's not sure if she can handle living in this town again with its oppressive familiarity, the painful memories of divorce and relationship breakdowns and heartbreak.

'Of course,' I tell her again. 'Of course I'll have you over for pizzas.'

My mother looks at me, her mouth pressed into a firm line. I make myself smile and wink at May. I'm rubbing my hands together to warm them.

'That's what Brian used to do with his hands,' my mother says, 'what you're doing right now. It's very effeminate.'

I emphasise the gesture and laugh, throwing a glance sideways at my daughter, who giggles back.

'You and Brian have a surprising amount in common,' my mother says. 'That's probably why you didn't get along.'

My hands stop. 'I'm nothing like Brian. There are plenty of reasons why we didn't get along. Besides which, whether I got along with him or not is hardly the point now, is it? I'm not the one that left him.'

My mother doesn't look at me anymore.

'I was just making a little joke,' she says. 'You shouldn't take yourself so seriously.'

After dinner, we walk side by side, through the backstreets of inner-city Newcastle. The sun has dropped and the cloud-ribbed sky is giving in to darkness. The air is hazy with salt. I think of how I lived for the first time in this neighbourhood as a ten-year-old boy. To one side, in a gloomy, cramped street full of narrow terraces, I can glimpse the house where my mother moved us after she'd left my first stepfather. The street hasn't changed much. The terraces look exactly the same. Twenty-five years have passed since it happened, but I can still imagine my stepfather there, out on the footpath, crowbar in hand, hammering at the door, demanding to be let in.

'He's a bastard,' my mother says suddenly. 'He's a bloody fucking bastard. I won't forget this.'

'What? Who?'

'The money. Brian.' She offers a helpless shrug. 'He's just relentless. He's like a vulture, circling around my life. I barely have enough money to survive, and he knows that, but still he puts this pressure on me. All that talk of love! Would you do that to someone you loved?'

I shake my head.

'No,' she says. 'That's not love.'

'Maybe you need to stop talking to him on the phone.'

My mother hugs her arms to her chest and gazes down to the cracked concrete of the footpath. 'He seems so alone. I feel for him, you know. I just feel so sorry for him.'

'If you talk to him every day, you're keeping him in your life. I feel like he's here in the house with us.'

She glances at me sideways, a shrewd look in her eye. 'Okay. I know what you're getting at. It's not as easy as you make out. One day, maybe, you'll see what it's like.'

I don't say anything.

She gives a short laugh. 'You'd think I'd be used to it, wouldn't you? The men in my life only ever take advantage of me. They just take. They don't understand how to give. Maybe men just don't.'

She drops her head and hobbles along faster. For a

long time, she used to walk faster than anyone I knew, and all I could do was try not to get left behind. But those days are probably gone for good. Now I have to slow down.

'Yes,' she mutters after a while. 'He's not the first man to take advantage of me.'

'Wait,' I say. 'Didn't you give Brian the money for yourself? For your own peace of mind?'

She doesn't answer straight away.

'That's right,' she tells me at last, her tone firming. 'That's right.'

We walk on in silence.

Over the years, Brian became increasingly frustrated with my brothers and me. It would come out in conversations with my mother, which she faithfully relayed to us in every detail. He said that we were too selfish and arrogant to learn from an older and wiser man, and that he had bent over backwards and practically grovelled for our sake. He had tried to educate us, to give us the father that we'd never had, and we had treated him with disdain, refused the hand of friendship. We were no better than his own children.

When my mother began to speak more often of her desire to leave, he said that she too had failed to learn anything from him.

'You desperately need to be taught a lesson,' he told her. 'I could teach you so much, and you're just going to walk away from all of that. It's tragic.'

'I know,' my mother said. 'I know.'

~

I used to visit them a bit on the Gold Coast, but in Myrtleford, I visited them only once. My mother wanted to see May for Christmas. On our arrival, after seven hours of travel, Brian ushered me straight back into his car.

'The men in the house need to go for a drive!' he declared to my mother and May. He clapped me on the back. 'Don't we?'

We drove up and down the main street and he pointed out the post office and a couple of cafes and then he drove to the outskirts of the town to the road sign that indicated its outskirts, where dense green paddocks full of cows stretched towards hills covered in pine trees, beyond them the quiet mountains, peaks edged in snow. He pressed a button and the windows slid down.

'So this is it,' he told me, 'the paradise in which your mother and I live.'

He waited. I told him it looked beautiful, and then neither of us said anything for a while.

'I could take you further if you like,' he said at last.

'That's all right,' I told him.

On the drive home, our car ran out of petrol. Despite how much he paid for the cars, Brian only ever put a small amount of fuel in the tank because he didn't want to spend too much money on the act of driving itself. The car broke down in strange places, though my mother didn't have the heart to tell him that she thought it was his fault. While we walked to the service station with a jerry can, Brian talked at length about his sense of mortality, the meaning of his life.

'I can't figure it out,' he said. 'I have all of this wisdom, this wealth of knowledge in my head that I want to share. There is so much I could teach people. I have come this far and I have no idea what to do next.'

I was thinking of all the stories my mother had been telling me about him for years, the intimate details that she had shovelled into my head so that I could understand what her life with him was like.

'Maybe,' I suggested at last, 'all you can do is enjoy the little things.'

The visit to Myrtleford was also the last time I saw Brian. Towards the end of my stay, his mood deteriorated and he got into a fight with my mother. It started over their dog, an old golden retriever. He'd bought her the dog as a present, but had started threatening to run off with it when my mother cooled on their relationship. Or kill it.

Now May wanted to hold the leash while they took the dog for a walk. Brian told her no.

'Why can't she walk the dog?' my mother asked. 'She's only here for a few days, for God's sake.'

'She needs to learn a few lessons,' Brian said. 'And if we don't start now, she could end up like you. You women need to be told *no* every now and again. Life isn't fair and we can't always get what we want. Now it just so happens that I want to hold the leash, and I have every right to hold the leash if that's what I feel like. I have more right to that than she does.'

'Don't be a child,' my mother said.

'You're putting her before me,' Brian said.

My mother clenched her fists and stared back at him. 'She's my granddaughter!'

We were standing on the street. I walked off with May, who was crying. I started tickling her to make her laugh. My mother and Brian talked some more. Then Brian threw the leash on the ground at her feet.

'I do this with an open heart!' he shouted and went back into the house.

The door slammed. I stared after him, more in wonder than anything else.

'I'm not putting up with this!' my mother said.

She followed him inside and told him to leave. She said that enough was enough and that she would be much happier without the misery that he put into her life. He said fine, that he wanted to go anyway, and he jumped into his car, revved it, and tore off down the road.

The next day, I got out of bed at the sound of his voice. Brian was standing in the hallway over my mother with his finger thrust in her face. In a breathy, rapid tone, he was telling her that it was shameful, what she'd done, telling an old man to leave his own house. He would never leave, not until she'd become a better person and accepted what he had to teach. The size of him, the way he hulked over my mother, even the beard, reminded me of my first stepfather. My daughter was hiding in her bedroom.

'Brian,' I said, stepping into the hallway, 'you need to calm down. You need to stop shouting. You're scaring my daughter.'

He turned on me with that rigid finger trembling between us. 'Don't you *dare* tell me what to do!'

My mother touched his shoulder. 'Please leave, Brian.'

'I won't!' he shouted. 'I'll *never* walk out that door.'

'Brian,' I said, 'listen to her. If a woman tells you to leave her house, you really should.'

Brian left in the end, to stay with his son who lived in the next town along. But the next day he came back and he approached me as I loaded the car ready for my trip back to the airport.

'How is the great orator going?' he asked.

I told him that I was fine. He moved between the car and me. There was hardly any space between us. He spoke in a low, rasping voice. 'I want you to know that you're an irrelevant prick and that I'm never going to listen to a word that you say ever again.'

His eyes widened fractionally as he said this, and then he lifted his fingers and thrust them into his ears.

'I'm not listening, I'm not listening, I'm not listening,' he chanted, his watery eyes unwavering on mine. He was wearing a golfer's cap with a red pompom on the top. The pompom shivered with each nod of his head. The tip of his nose was pink with fury. I looked at him for a moment, and then walked back inside.

'He's fine,' my mother assured me with a weary smile. 'I know how to handle men like him.'

~

Four weeks have passed since she's left him and Myrtleford for good, and my mother and I are house hunting, driving along the streets of Newcastle from one inspection to another.

'Newcastle just doesn't change, does it?' she says wearily. 'No matter how much it changes.'

I stare straight ahead and turn up the radio. 'In some ways.'

My mother is depressed but trying to keep her spirits up. We are driving along Stewart Avenue, past one of the many streets in which we used to live, Alexander Street. On the left, beneath a gloom of figs and gum trees, is one of my old primary schools, Hamilton South. On the corner of the next street along from our old street stands a house that is mainly hidden by a high, dark green fence.

'It's for sale,' I say.

'What?'

'Nikki's house.'

'Oh,' she says.

The other day, I wandered through the house on the internet. I looked at all the rooms, which are done up, almost unrecognisable. The floors are freshly polished, the walls are painted white. If a family still lives there, they clean up well after themselves. The house is behind us now, and Mum doesn't look back.

'I miss her,' she says suddenly. 'Every Christmas, I think of her again. It was worse when I lived here, though. Much worse. You know, a city just becomes the memories you have of it.'

We both fall silent. While Nikki was my closest childhood friend, his mother, Susan, had been my mother's best friend, although that didn't really occur to me at the time. Nikki and Susan both died in a bus crash, along with Nikki's father and thirty-two other people. This happened three days before Christmas, and six days before the Newcastle earthquake, when I was fourteen. They are gone, and yet the house that they once lived in looks the same from the outside, and you can almost pretend they still live there. The only missing thing is the mulberry tree that once stood in the backyard. It's been killed off like most of the mulberry trees in Newcastle. I've walked past once or twice as an adult and leaned against the fence with my cheek. You can still hear the hum of the pool filter on the other side.

'They weren't happy, you know,' my mother says.

'Who?'

'Susan and Paul. They'd been living apart for a while and they'd just got back together for the trip to see their family in Newcastle.'

'I never noticed that they weren't happy.'

'Of course you didn't. You were too young.'

It's hard figuring out how or why people stay together sometimes. I never understood how Brian and my mother stayed together for so long. Emily tells me that there is usually a payoff when two people stay together, that each of them must get something out of it. If you can't see it, you're probably not looking closely enough.

My mother used to tell me that someone always has to play the hero, in every relationship. She played the hero with Brian. When you play the hero, you are the one that forgives and that lets things slide. The hero rises above the flaws of other people.

I started hearing from my mother about being the hero after my divorce from May's mother. It was only May and me back then, and my mother started coming during holidays to stay with us. May always looked forward to her arrival. We'd go on day trips. She'd get spoiled. My mother had always wished for a daughter of her own. If the three of us went to the movies, May would bring along a pillow for my mother, for her bad back. They slept in the same room together and May would wake her up in the middle of the night to have conversations with her. But my mother always stayed longer than I wanted her to, and I'd always feel my life getting tangled up in hers. I'd feel as if I was drowning.

This time around, May thinks it's great that my mother is staying with no end in sight.

'She has it good,' my mother says, over a glass of wine, after I've read May her stories for the night and she's asleep. 'Such a happy girl, and no wonder, really. I wish that I'd had it half as good as her. No one ever read *me* stories every night. No one ever made me feel so special or looked after my best interests in the way that people do for her. They still don't.'

My mother stares down at the ground and somewhere past it. 'When I was her age, I remember visiting my grandmother.'

She is talking about a woman I've never met but have heard a lot about, a woman that supported the Dutch resistance in World War II—though her son, my grandfather, was a collaborator.

'I saw her just once,' my mother murmurs. 'My father took me there on the back of his motorbike. We got to the town early and we went to the nearby forest where my father used to play as a boy, and we lay side by side on this mossy ground. My father told me that if I closed my eyes, fairies would come out around me. I closed my eyes and heard his breath, and I imagined all the fairies around us.

It's the only time that I can remember being close to him. Anyway, when we went to my grandmother's house, I had to stand to one side. I wasn't even offered a chair. My grandmother was very wealthy, she had servants and a huge house. She had this silver bowl full of expensive chocolates. The only time that she looked at me for the hour or so that we were there was when she took out one of those chocolates, unwrapped it, and fed it to her dog.'

She falls silent. I want to lean over, touch her hand like I used to when I was young.

'The children carry the sins of the parents,' she says softly.

'What?'

'My grandmother said that about us. Maybe she was right in some way. Maybe that's why it's still so hard for me now.'

I cross my legs and lean back in my chair. 'Well, May has a good life. You and I may have a complicated relationship, but with your granddaughter, it is simple and beautiful. That's something positive to focus on.'

'Yes,' my mother says, brightening a little, 'yes, it is. She's the best parts of both of us.'

We clink our glasses together and drink.

The next morning, as I am getting out my breakfast, my mother hobbles into the kitchen.

'Would you like a cup of tea?'

I smile back at her. 'No thanks. Can I make you one?'

'That's all right, Michael.'

I feel her still hovering at my back. She puts a hand on my shoulder as I am making my cup of coffee.

'You know, I'm really sorry,' she says.

'For what?'

'I'm sorry that you think we have a complicated relationship.' There is a sudden accusing glint in her eyes.

'Don't all adult children have a complicated relationship with their parents?'

My mother's face does not change and she walks away.

My mother says that it's the pain from her back that prevents her from sleeping, that keeps her moving around the house at night, and now we can add to that the fracture in her ankle that she acquired on a recent trip to Melbourne. The broken ankle increases her restlessness and makes her move around more, and the movement makes the broken ankle worse.

'Perhaps it is a sign,' my mother says as she stares down at it.

'Of what?' I ask her.

'You know, that I made the wrong decision in leaving Brian.'

'I think the universe has better things to do than punish you for leaving Brian.'

'Yes,' my mother says, 'maybe you're right.'

~

After I left Myrtleford with my daughter, my mother smoothed things over with Brian. She blamed Christmas, the heat, her back. She apologised for telling him to leave the house and apologised on my behalf, too. Brian forgave her although he assured her that he wouldn't forget. He never forgave *me*, though. He would sit on the corner of her bed some nights and cry with his head in his hands and tell my mother that it had been the most humiliating experience of his life, being told to leave the house by a young man.

But I wasn't the one that had told him to leave, I said to my mother.

'I know,' she'd answer. 'But *he* thinks you were.'

If I phoned up my mother and Brian answered, he wouldn't say a word to me, no matter how polite I was. He would simply pass the phone to my mother and say, 'It's the arsehole.'

'I do feel bad, though,' my mother tells me now, reflecting back on all of that. 'I think that maybe I turned you against him. I think that I talked too much about him, and maybe that's too much pressure to put on your children. Words and stories can be dangerous. Maybe I made him sound worse than he really was.'

'Maybe you did,' I admit. 'I never know what I'm supposed to do with the information.'

My mother nods. 'I guess that I should tell you more

of the good things. When I used to wake up in distress from the pain in my back or the nightmares, he'd make me a cup of tea and he'd rub my legs for hours when they got sore. You don't know how many nights he did that.'

'You're right, I don't.'

We stare at one another in silence.

'But there were always the inconsistencies,' she goes on, 'to keep me from really feeling good around him. I felt very controlled in all that, constantly off balance. Each morning he would get up and say, "I love you… *today*." Or sometimes he'd say, "I *like* you, today." It was like a weather report. But I felt safe with him. I knew that he would never leave me. And out of all the men in my life, he was probably the kindest. Don't you think?'

Back to this word, hospitality. If you delve deeper into its origins, beyond Latin, to the European languages that came before, 'hospitality' has its roots in the words *ghos*, meaning 'guest', and *poti*, meaning 'master' or 'powerful'. And maybe, when you put all of this together, it means that in order to be hospitable to your guests, you need to have the power *to get rid of them* in the first place.

In some ways, my mother looked after the men in her life very well, but I am still not sure that she could ever be hospitable to them. All I know is that, for many years, I lived there too. I lived there with her for longer than I thought. When you are used to motion, leaving is at once the easiest and the most difficult thing in the world.

My mother ended up leaving my house after five weeks. When I dropped her at the train station, she sadly touched my face and told me to look after myself. Then she left for Sydney to stay with Con. She called me a week later.

'Hello, Mike,' she said. 'It's Mum.'

She said her name with an inflection at the end, as if she were posing a question.

I asked her how she was.

'I don't know what my next move will be,' she answered. We both waited. The phone hissed softly between us. 'I don't know whether I will try to find a place in Newcastle after all. I didn't feel so good there. It's best sometimes to move on. Maybe I'll go to the Gold Coast. I've even been thinking of Myrtleford again.'

'I guess you have to do what you have to do.'

She gave a sigh. 'It's all up to me now that I've left Brian.'

I remained silent.

'And how are things with you, Michael?' she asked.

'I'm fine.'

'Are you sure?'

'Yes.'

The silence expanded between us once more.

'A mother,' she said, 'can worry for her sons, you know.'

'I know,' I told her.

A few weeks later she left a message on my answering machine. Her voice had an arthritic edge of cheerfulness. You could almost mistake it for hope. She'd moved to Albury, which was not so far away from Myrtleford. I had to come for a visit sometime. She gave me Brian's mobile number in case I needed to contact her for anything.

We didn't talk for a long time after that.

Sometimes in the middle of the night, I have nightmares. I've had them since I was a child. I wake up afterwards and forget that I am an adult. For a moment I am terrified of the darkness, too terrified to move. I speak in a rush and my words don't make sense. I am a stranger inside my own body. When this happens, Emily touches my shoulder and tells me to go back to sleep. But I make myself get out of bed and walk through the house without turning on the lights, the cold seeping through the floorboards under my feet and resting on my neck.

I check on my daughter. I go downstairs and make sure the elephant is facing the door. Emily calls softly to me again from our bedroom, but I keep walking, up and down, up and down, in the darkness, on the creaking floor, feeling the pressure and give beneath my bare feet, hearing the wind and the ocean outside. I have to do this to remind myself that I am a grown-up, and that the house is now my own.

Acknowledgements

I am deeply grateful to Keri Glastonbury for her invaluable insight and support over the course of this book; to Rebecca Starford for her fantastic editing and her enthusiasm for the work; to Martin Hughes for believing in the value of the stories; to Scott Brewer, who read and commented on the various drafts of this work tirelessly and was there with his brilliant mind, friendship, guitar, and occasionally, even a ute and various gardening implements; to my fellow writers, David Kelly, Ryan O'Neill and Patrick Cullen, who have each, in their own way, helped me to arrive at this point; to Ben Matthews for telling me to write; to Charlotte Wood, who gave me my first break; to Cate Kennedy, who has been an inspiring example and wonderful supporter of me, as she has been for many other writers; to Raimond Gaita and Debra Adelaide for their generous endorsements; to my daughter, for motivating me to get started; to my mother and brothers for the journey we shared, and the things they made me see in the world and in myself; to my wife, Kimiko, for her unwavering love and the beauty she brings to my life.

I am also indebted to the University of Newcastle, particularly the School of Humanities and Social Sciences, for the critical funding and support that it has provided to me over the years.

Different versions of two chapters in this book have been previously published. Chapter 9 appeared under the title 'The Men Outside My Room', in *The Best Australian Stories 2011*. Chapter 10 appeared under the title 'Like My Father, My Brother', in the anthology *Brothers and Sisters*.